Possessive

Hostages #7

Alexis Abbott

If you want to be notified of my latest books, join my
newsletter!
http://alexisabbott.com/newsletter

For a full list of cw/tw for this title, please visit my
website:
http://alexisabbott.com

CHAPTER 1

ZAKHAR

Becoming *Obshchak* in the Bratva had cut into my play time.

But I know as well as anyone that too much tension can make even the most disciplined man snap. To maintain control, to be the strong fist of the *Pakhan*, I would have to force myself to do the one thing I've been neglecting: Have a relaxing night out, in a private place, away from any prying eyes of friends and foes alike.

I had taken the winding descent into the belly of the deceptively deteriorating building countless times, but the past few months, my journeys to the *Velvet Kiss Lounge* had become scarce. It was one of the few places I enjoyed, nestled into a back alley that you'd never find if you didn't know what you were looking for. The club was its own secret little world, the place where big shots came to pretend they had an edge, swirling cocktails on high-backed velvet loveseats.

For a guy like me, it was puff pastry soft, but everyone needs an escape once in a while.

The deep, thumping bass music prickles my skin pleasantly beneath my heavy leather jacket as I take in my surroundings, glancing over the large dance floor in the center of the space as it pulses with sweat-slicked bodies.

I make my way to the bar and see a familiar face. I don't even have to order before he has a glass of top-shelf vodka poured, and the bottle set on the counter beside it.

"It's on the house! My boss wanted to thank you for last time."

Last time was four months ago, when I'd bloodied my knuckles on the face of some pimp looking to drug a girl's drink. The bouncers hadn't seen it, but I had. I glance around and I notice there's a few new faces, dressed all in black, looking like elegant thugs.

I nod at the bartender, accepting the offering.

"Glad to see he took my suggestion to up staffing seriously," I replied. I remember fondly the fear in the owner's eyes when I told him it was his fault for trying to cut corners on security.

"We've had to do a half dozen training sessions on spotting sexual assault since then," the bartender said, knowing better than to sound disgruntled. I give him a long stare, and once he shrinks away, I head to my post at the end of the long bar counter along the back wall.

My gaze flicks up to the gaudy golden mirror nestled on the wall opposite me, positioned between two shelves of booze. I meet my own reflection, still and stoic in the dim light. I know I'm a good-looking man, with my high cheekbones and my strong jaw. Not to mention my powerful, hulking frame. I stand nearly six-foot-four, with the broad chest and shoulders of a bodybuilder.

My muscles are not put on for show, however.

I am not one of the many pretty boys here in the Velvet Kiss tonight, pawing at pretty girls for attention. I don't have to subject myself to gain a woman's attention, nor her desire.

In fact, as I sit here, I lose count of the number of women who stare at me, blushing and stunned, from across the room. It's like clockwork: a girl notices me and loses interest in the man speaking to her. He turns to see who or what is distracting his prey, only to find me. One look at my intimidating size and expression, and the man cuts his losses.

Better to lose out on a one-night-stand than to lose a fight with me.

I don't even have to get up from my post. But tonight, I'm not interested.

It has all become so routine, these flings. That's another reason why I haven't been here in so long. It's no longer satisfying to roll the dice on finding a woman in the crowd who can keep up with me, using her as a crass way to relieve tension.

The path I walk is lonely, but it is also dangerous. I won't bring a woman into my world unless I'm sure I can push her back out of it… or perhaps if she is strong enough to survive it.

It's not vanity that brings me to this spot before the mirror, rather, it's a strategic means of viewing the entire club without ever having to turn around.

It's part of my training. The instinct to find the cleanest view in the house.

I need to have my finger on the pulse of what's happening around me, even when I'm supposed to be off duty.

But the reality is that a man like me is never fully off the clock. Even now, even here, I am always watching. Waiting for the moment to defend or strike as the situation demands. While the other patrons lose their inhibitions, I hold tight to my own. I prefer the darkness, and I seek it out, but that doesn't mean I'm safe from what lurks in the shadows for me.

I pour myself another drink, my heart keeping rhythm with the pulsing music, and it begins to massage away the aches of several grueling months. Change never comes easy, I imagine, but that goes double for the Mafia. My promotion hadn't been without challenges, and rising to Obshchak had bristled a few spines.

Nothing I can't handle, but I was certainly noticing the weight of it as I tried to force myself into a state of relative relaxation.

But fate had other ideas.

I glance down as the long golden hour hand of my wrist watch ticks to twelve, and when my dark eyes return to the bar, I see an angel.

The girl is absolutely stunning. She could barely be eighteen, except for the drink in her hand. Her long, blonde hair is as straight as a pin, which falls just past her shoulders and frames her heart-shaped, pretty face. Her eyes are large and luminous, her lips like a pink rosebud.

She wears a tight black dress that clings to her ample curves and barely reaches the middle of her thigh. The dress is low-cut in the front, showing a devastating amount of cleavage. When she turns around for a moment, I see a similar plunge in the back.

The young girl stands out among the glittering crowds of gorgeous women here tonight. She practically glows.

Rage boils up in me when I see a group of four young men swarm around her.

I'm already on my feet when she slips away from their leering propositions, briskly walking down the hall to the restrooms.

I smile to myself. Smart girl. She's made her first attempt at an escape. I make eye contact with a bouncer across the room who had been watching as well, and nod in a mutual understanding and respect.

The respect dims once I realize that the men are still skulking around, waiting for her to come out.

The bouncers should be acting now, removing them before it becomes something more serious. I'm storming over to tell them just that when I see the girl cautiously poke her head around the corner from the hallway.

She tiptoes out of the hallway and slips into the writhing mass of people on the dance floor, clearly hoping to disappear into the crowd. She's short enough to lose herself in the group, but unfortunately, she doesn't consider the fact that her pursuers are tall enough to track her. I watch them point her out to each other with determined looks on their faces. They're angry. Offended that this girl has the audacity to give them the slip. And she has no idea they're coming right for her.

Instinct kicks in and I sink into the dancing crowd with my eyes locked on the blonde girl.

From the other side of the bar, the four frat guys are pushing toward her, too.

All around me, the bodies twist and undulate against each other. I push a path through the dance floor and manage to reach the girl just as the other men do. I see the momentary confusion and fear in her beautiful blue-green eyes as she looks at me, then back at them. I give her the faintest of nods and put my hand on the small of her back. As soon as my fingers touch her, I feel her body relax a little.

"Act natural," I whisper to her. She leans toward me as the men look us up and down, sneers on their drunken faces. It's not a look I see often, and it's almost amusing, if not for the very real fear that I know is cooling the girl's blood.

"Did you find the bathroom okay?" I ask her, my gaze still fiercely locked on the men. They're frozen in place, eyes wide like they've just been cornered by a rabid wolf.

I stare them down as she murmurs, "Uh-huh."

"Did anyone give you any trouble?" I ask, with a sharp edge to my voice.

"No trouble here, man," one of the guys says, hands up in surrender.

"Yeah, we were just leaving," adds his buddy.

I give them a cold smile, still not blinking. "Good choice. Have a safe evening, boys."

They look chilled to the bone as they slink away, tails between their legs. Before they even leave the pit, the bouncer is finally there to see them escorted out.

The young woman looks up at me with her eyes shining. She gives me an exhilarated smile, and I decide in that instant to take her home with me. She isn't their prey tonight.

She's mine.

"How can I thank you?" she asks, tucking her hair behind her ear.

"Dance with me," I command softly, and slip my arm around her waist.

"Oh," she gasps as our bodies press together.

But she quickly warms to my touch, seeming to melt into my arms as we sway. The music pulses underneath us, the crimson lights beaming across our faces. The girl reaches up to put her arms around my neck, her fingertips brushing against the dark hair at the nape of my neck. A chill of pure desire rolls down my spine. My cock stirs to life.

I can feel her heartbeat racing faster with every spin, every time our eyes lock together. Her body is so soft and smooth against me as my hands slowly move down to grope her ass. I push her into me, feeling every swell of her curves.

The clock ticks on, inching closer to morning. I decide I'm finished with the club scene for the evening. I have other, grander plans for the two of us.

"Come home with me," I growl in her ear.

She swallows hard, blinking up at me with those big blue eyes. She's a trembling soft flower on the verge of bloom, and I intend to be the one to pluck her tonight. All for myself. She slips her hand into mine and stands on tiptoe to lean toward my ear.

CHAPTER 2

HARTLEY

I inhale his heady masculine scent. It fills my nose and lungs, going straight to my brain like some kind of irresistible drug. I feel dizzy on my heels, tottering in the capable, powerful arms of my savior. I haven't even had that much to drink tonight. Only a single vodka cranberry, sipped over the course of nearly two hours. I didn't come here to get wasted and make bad decisions. It was my goal to lie low tonight, just enjoy a casual evening of sipping my drink and people-watching. It's free entertainment: sitting on the sidelines while all these strangers dance, talk, laugh, and fall in love over the DJ's grinding beat.

I suppose somewhere in the very back of my mind, in that locked drawer where I keep the memories and desires I can't touch, there's a part of me who wanted to find that here, too.

Lust. Intrigue.

Maybe a dash of measured danger.

After all, I'm not any better than these folks around me.

Just because I have to fit my whole world into a space small enough to keep my secret safe doesn't mean the desire goes away. I'm a hot-blooded twenty-one-year-old running feral in the big city. These streets should be my playground, this club should be my lair.

Too bad those four frat brats had to interrupt my evening and force me out of my hiding spot.

Right into the willing, protective arms of this man towering over me.

We're in the center of the packed dance floor, but we might as well be all by ourselves. The music, the smell of sweat, the cocoon of body heat around us—it shrinks back in comparison to the intensity of this man's presence. I know from the moment he first locked eyes with me, he is in control. His deep growl of a voice, his fingers on the small of my back, and the way he so easily cowed those four troublemakers prove that beyond a shadow of a doubt. This ridiculously handsome, enigmatic stranger holds me in the palm of his hand.

I'm at his mercy… and I like it.

I rest my hand on his shoulder for balance as I wobble on tiptoe to answer his command.

"I'm all yours," I murmur softly, the syllables ticklish on my lips as they brush against the shell of his ear.

I'm almost surprised by the words I'm saying. I don't make split-second decisions in the dark like this. I'm careful. I keep to myself. The last thing I planned to do tonight is go home with an intimidating stranger. Even if he *is* the most handsome man I've ever seen, and his touch makes me weak in the knees.

But something tells me there's no use denying this man anything.

Especially when I want it so badly, too.

I have been so patient. I have waited so long.

God knows my dreams have been filled with flashes of bare skin, hot hands, and eager tongues. I fall into a fantasy every time I close my eyes, and this man looks like the combination of every mysterious suitor I've ever dreamed up. But better. Because instead of living in the unreachable depths of my mind, he is *real*. Blood, flesh, bone.

When he slips his hand around mine, I know I would follow him anywhere.

"Let's go," he instructs in a gruff whisper.

I am amazed at the way he parts the crowd as we make our way off the bustling dance floor. The crowd thins out, forming a path for us. Men and women watch us with envy, with awe. We make a striking pair, and I can't believe I'm the one lucky enough to go home with this man. His fingers burn against my skin, and I feel tingly from my head to my toes just being near him. My heart races faster and harder with every step we take toward the staircase. It hits me that I am about to be all alone with this stranger. He could snap me like a twig if he wanted.

That familiar alarm bell sounds in the back of my mind.

Danger ahead. I don't know him.

I don't know his intentions.

And yet, as we climb the winding staircase up to the street level, my desire outweighs my fear. I'm desperate to find out what comes next. What will he do to me?

How will it feel?

My suitor and the doorman exchange silent nods and we step out into the balmy summer night. It's late July in

New York City. An occasional breeze rolls by to mediate the heat, but with this man standing next to me, I can't cool down. The narrow alleyway is empty and quiet save for the sounds of traffic on either side of the block.

Before I can open my mouth to ask where we're going, the dark-eyed man takes both of my wrists in his hands. With one smooth movement, he walks me back against the wall, pinning my hands over my head. My chest rises and falls rapidly, my eyes wide with surprise. The man looks me up and down with hungry eyes. He licks his lips, and I can tell he likes what he sees. In the dim streetlight, I can see the sharp cut of his cheekbones and his angular jaw. His eyes are dark and deep. I have to look away before I lose myself in them. When I turn my head, he dips down to nuzzle into my hair above my ear. I tense up as he breathes in my scent and presses the hard length of his body into mine. I let out a soft sigh of desire when I feel his cock twitch against my pelvis. Like a reflex, I arch my back to press into his erection.

He groans in approval, his lips trailing down from my ear to my cheek and down to my mouth. He stops there for a second, just waiting. Teasing me. I part my lips, barely daring to breathe. A devilish smile slowly spreads across his face, those dark eyes boring hard into mine. He can see my soul, I feel it. He knows the shadowy things I crave. He looks straight into that most shameful, secret part of me and finds exactly what he's looking for.

He leans in and captures my lips in a fierce kiss. It's like something forbidden opens up inside of me. I moan into the kiss, going limp in his arms. My heart pounds like crazy. My palms sweat, pinned against the brick wall. My body burns hotter and hotter, impatient for this man to show me the way. I have never been kissed like this before.

And then, just as quickly as it began, he pulls back. I pout, my body straining toward his. He looks pleased with himself, with his catch of the evening. I've passed the test.

"Why did you—" I begin, but he stops me with a finger to my lips.

He shakes his head and starts to walk away in long, confident strides.

For a moment I stare after him in confusion. Then, not wanting to be left behind, I run after him. As if he expected this, he takes my hand and leads me down the block to a big black luxury sedan, glossy under the neon lights. There's the jingle of keys, and then he tips me into the passenger seat and shuts the door. He slides behind the wheel and starts the engine. The black car pulls away from the curb and takes off down the back streets, hurtling in the direction of Brooklyn. I'm completely enraptured by my mysterious, sexy savior. Or captor? At this point, I can't tell the difference. All I know is that I can't resist him. If he wants me, he can have me. I'm at his mercy.

As he drives, he reaches over to squeeze my thigh with one strong hand. I suck in a tight breath. His fingers trace my inner thigh, teasing my skin through the thin black fabric of my dress. Every few minutes, he moves his hand up another fraction of an inch. Every time, it sends my mind into a frenzy of lust. My pussy tingles between my legs. I'm aching for him.

I steal glances over at him in the darkness. The overhead lights pass across his sharp, handsome features. I wonder who he is, what he does. For some reason, I'm afraid to even ask his name. I lose track of time and place. It could have been an hour or ten minutes, I'm too distracted to care.

By the time the car rolls to a stop outside a detached loft apartment building, I'm raring to go. He cuts the engine and slips out to take my hand and lead me up to his front door. It takes him just a second with the key, and then we're inside. I hear a digital beeping sound as he types some code into a security system on the wall next to the door.

I barely have time to admire his swanky apartment before he cups my face in his hands and kisses me again. This time, his tongue pushes into my mouth. His hands smooth down my shoulders and around to my back. He deftly unzips my black dress and I gasp against his lips at the sensation of his fingertips on my bare spine. The dress slides down my body, revealing my breasts barely restrained in a strapless bra. My suitor gathers my thick hair in one hand and gently pulls my head to one side. He dives in to kiss and lightly bite my exposed neck, making me whimper with need. The sensations roll down my whole body as he slips the dress down to the floor. His hands grope my ass and he gently snaps the tight elastic waistband of my black lacy thong.

This is not the type of girl I am.

But from the second I saw him, I knew that my life was never going to be the same.

That I was never going to be the same.

I shudder at the sting of light pain. Goosebumps pop up on my skin, betraying how good it feels. He gives my ass a hard, resounding smack. I gasp and tilt my head back. The sharp pain excites me, and he kisses down my throat and between my tits, his tongue teasing my skin. His hands grasp my narrow waist and smooth around the swell of my hips. He rocks against me, letting me feel how hard he is. My mouth waters. I'm aching to be filled. To be fucked by this mysterious, dangerous man.

He's the type of guy I should be avoiding. The type that could tug me back into the dark and seedy parts of the world that I was trying to get away from. Yet I find myself completely unable to resist him.

For just one night, I'm going to succumb to my base desires.

"Who are you?" I hear myself whisper between gasps of delight.

He lets out a low growl, but doesn't answer. He steps back a little and lets his hand slide up my body to my neck. I freeze up, just watching him while his large hand slowly, gently tightens around my throat. He presses in at the sides to constrict my air flow without really hurting me. Yet.

This is definitely when I should be running for the door. You don't go home with a stranger and let him wrap his hands around your neck. That's, like, rule number one for hookups.

And yet as I stare into his eyes, I see myself reflected in the near black of his iris, and I don't look afraid.

His other hand comes up next to my face, but then he snaps his fingers and glances down at the floor.

I understand instantly what he wants me to do. It's instinctual, like some animal part of me coming alive at his beckoning. He's speaking a language to me that I never thought I knew, and yet he knows I'm fluent.

With his hand still bound around my throat, I slowly

kneel down in front of him. My heart feels like it's about to burst. I gaze up at my captor with pure surrender.

He stares down at me, unflinching. From down here, he looks even more terrifyingly in control than ever. I try to swallow, but it aches with his hand around my neck. His thumb gently strokes my throat, then his hand moves up to cup my chin. He holds it there, forcing me to keep his gaze.

I know he can see the desire plain on my face. He understands what he does to me, what he awakens in me. We've hardly spoken a full sentence between us, and yet, I have the strange feeling that every path I've ever taken in my life has led up to this moment. To our chance meeting at the Velvet Kiss Lounge.

"I am your master," he says, finally answering my question. "And you are my pet."

If any other man said those words to me, I'd go nuclear. I've made it a priority in my life not to belong to anyone but myself. But when he says it, I feel a trickle of warm, wet honey drip down my legs. My thighs are sticky with my own juices, my pussy drooling for him to touch it.

He grabs my face in his hands, squeezing tighter as his eyes flash with danger.

"I can relieve that ache inside you," he growls. "I can feed your desire until you're full."

"Please," I mutter breathlessly.

"But only if you accept my terms," he went on, never breaking eye contact.

"Anything," I gasp.

There's no trace of play when he says: "You will agree to obey my every command."

I feel it—the crossroads. My answer determines my fate. But I feel just as strongly that there is no other reply. Nothing to say to him, except…

"Yes." My voice sounds stronger than I feel. "I will obey."

CHAPTER 3

ZAKHAR

I smile down at the beautiful, desperate woman caught tight in my grasp. Her skin is silky smooth under my fingertips. Her bone structure is so delicate, her chin so tiny between my finger and thumb.

When I touched her throat before, I felt her pulse flutter like the wings of a frightened dove. Even now, I can almost hear her heart beating. I can nearly see it pumping in her chest, making those full breasts rise and fall.

When I look closer, I see that the young woman is trembling with desire, tinged with an edge of fear, no doubt. I know the kind of effect I have on women. She's a little afraid, and she's right to be. I'm a dangerous man, and I deal in dangerous matters.

But she's also intrigued, caught up in my seductive game, though I can tell that this is new to her.

It's obvious that I've already won her over, but I have to be certain.

"You understand what you're agreeing to?" I prompt her.

I feel her swallow hard, her mouth going dry at my question. But I know as well as she does that there's no going back. I have given her a taste of what I can show her. Now, she is bound to me. She's desperate to find out how far I will go, how far I can push her. As much as it scares her, she can't look away. That lust she's been clamping down on won't let her. Fear is a powerful force, but true desire outpaces fear every time.

I don't know her story, but I can see the shadows of it following her. There are two types of women who would thrill at this level of risk. The first type is those that have lived a boring life, devoid of excitement, and in desperate need of a quick rush.

She is the second type.

The type who has been forged in fear and fire, who has been twisted by the pain of the world. For her, there can never be a normal life. She will always be trying to control those powerful feelings inside of her that threaten everything she knows and loves.

We have that in common.

I can teach her what she needs to know, as long as she's strong enough to face the darkness lurking within her.

Within me.

"I have to do as you say," she whispers.

I nod slowly, letting my hand slip from her chin up to the top of her head. I stroke her soft, golden hair and she pushes into my hand. Her big blue eyes roll shut as she enjoys the feel of my fingers combing through her hair. A little sweetness can go a long way, I've learned.

"You don't *have* to do anything," I remind her in a low growl, "but yes, you will."

I brush my fingers across her full bottom lip. So soft, so plush.

"Because you want this more than anything, don't you?" I inquire.

She nods eagerly and I press my thumb between her lips. She allows it with no hesitation, her eyes never breaking contact with mine. To my delight, I feel her tongue flick over my thumb, and then she sucks on it, a soft moan vibrating through her throat. My cock twitches in response.

"You are a toy for me," I explain, "a pretty plaything designed for my pleasure."

She stares at me attentively, like an innocent student on the first day of class. Like she's angling for a good grade and some extra credit. I will see how far she's willing to go for that. I pop my thumb out of her mouth and she licks her lips.

"What is your name?" I ask her.

I see a flicker of panic pass over her eyes. The gears turning in her mind. For a moment, I assume she is going to lie to me. In fact, her hesitation tells me that she probably makes a habit of lying—at least about her name. What is this beautiful little creature hiding?

But when she softly answers, "Hartley," I realize instantly it's the truth. She sounds a little shy, like she's divulging something scandalous. She doesn't offer a surname, but I don't need one.

"Hartley," I repeat, enjoying the feel of the syllables on my tongue. "A pretty name. As for me, you can call me Master."

Her cheeks flush rosy pink and her eyes dart away. I grab her face in my hand so she has to look at me when I tell her emphatically, "You will call me Master. You will trust and obey. I am going to push you to your limits, Miss Hartley, but if you would ever like me to stop, all you have to do is say the word *nyet*. Repeat it for me now."

"*Nyet*," she mumbles awkwardly. It doesn't come naturally to her, but she does as she's told. She's eager to please me. My cock stirs again, pulsing with need.

"Good girl," I tell her.

I snap my fingers for her to stand up. She does so instantly and awaits her next command. I gesture for her to walk in front of me, up the staircase to the loft bedroom. Hartley slowly walks to the stairs, looks back at me, and then begins to ascend. I follow her, admiring the view of her ample ass from behind, jiggling with every step. The barely-there string of her panties slides between those juicy cheeks, just begging to be snapped. Her straight blonde hair swishes from side to side, and every now and again I get a glimpse of her glorious breasts from the side, barely restrained in that black strapless bra. Her long, toned legs end in a pair of black pumps, which click on the hardwood steps.

Halfway up the staircase, I suddenly grab her waist from behind and bend her over the railing. She yelps in surprise, but I catch both arms behind her back, holding her there while I feel her up. I let my hands rove up and down her smooth, nubile body. I press my cock against her supple ass and grind into her. I pull my hand back and deliver a hard smack to her behind that makes her cry out. For a second, there's a red-hot handprint there, and I watch it quickly fade. I lean in close to whisper in her ear.

"Keep going."

I back up and let her gather herself, then follow her the

rest of the way up. The loft bedroom is dark, illuminated only dimly by the glow of the moon through the skylight. It forms a patch of almost eerie white light on my king-sized bed. Hartley stands still, looking around in the low light. I step past her to sit on the end of the bed. She starts to walk toward me and I hold up my hand. She halts instantly, looking a little put out.

I give her a sly smile. "Don't worry, princess. You're coming too. First, take everything off. Strip for me," I command.

Hartley reaches back to unclasp her strapless bra. She drops it to the floor and her beautiful tits fall free. My fingertips crave to touch those perky, perfect breasts. She gently kicks off her black heels, bringing her down a couple inches. And then, with her blue eyes trained on me, she strips out of her black lacy thong. She makes no attempt to cover herself with her hands. I admire the blonde, downy curls above her flower, and my cock stiffens even more when I see the shiny, sticky juices between her thighs. She's dripping for me, ready to be devoured.

But not yet. She must learn how to please me first.

"Get down on your knees," I instruct her.

"Yes, Master," she says, and kneels down on the floor. God, she's perfect.

I curl my finger, beckoning for her to come to me. She understands what I desire. With her eyes locked on me and her taut ass poking up in the air, the beautiful young woman crawls across the floor to me on all fours. When she stops in front of me, I stroke her hair with one hand while the other unzips my black pants. Hartley's pretty mouth is watering. Her eyes are wide with longing. I take out my massive, stiff cock, stroking its length in front of her face. I gather a fistful of her silky hair and pull her head back. Obediently, she opens her mouth and splays out her tongue for me. Unable to resist any longer, I shove my cock between her plush lips.

"Fuck, yes," I growl, cupping the back of her head.

I buck my hips and hold her in place, letting my full length spear down her throat. Hartley gags for a moment, her pretty eyes watering. Saliva rolls down her chin. But I give her no mercy, and she quickly regains her composure, sucking my cock with renewed vigor. Her smooth, warm tongue slides up and down the sensitive underside, flicking around the tip as I push into her mouth again and again. Before long, I'm fully fucking her face, my balls slapping against her chin as she chokes on my cock.

"That's right. Take your Master's cock," I grunt through gritted teeth.

"Mmmph," she moans, and sucks harder.

I feel a flash of intense, mind-numbing pleasure—a warning. This sexy little thing has me on the edge of coming already. But not yet. I have more to show her.

I pull her hair, yanking her back from my cock with a wet slurping sound. She looks dazed, drunk on dick. My member is swollen and aching. I know what I want, and I'm done waiting around for it. I scoop Hartley up and toss her on the bed. I climb atop her, grabbing hold of both her arms. She looks up at me in hazy confusion as I secure her wrists to the black post headboard with ties in the bedside drawer.

"You're mine," I hiss.

"Yours," she repeats softly.

I dip down to kiss her. Our lips crash together hard. I

lightly bite her bottom lip, making her moan. I reach down to wrench her thighs wider apart, tugging down my pants to position my cock at her slick, clenching hole. I tease her by sliding the thick head around that sensitive band of nerves at her opening. She moans and pushes up into me, begging for more. I slide my cock up and down the length of her dewy flower, paying special attention to her clit. She shivers underneath me, and I can tell she's on the verge.

So I pull back for a moment, refusing to touch her. Hartley whimpers and strains toward me, but her bound wrists won't let her reach for me. She lifts her hips, her eyes wide and watering with desire. The girl is desperate for me to fuck her.

"Please," she murmurs breathlessly. "Please."

I position my cock at her entrance again, pressing just enough to tease her. I can feel her twitching. One little push and she'll be done for. This time, I need it too. I grab her hips with both hands and hold her in place. I rear back, then plunge my cock deep inside of her in one forceful motion.

"Ohh!" she cries out, writhing as her cunt clenches around my thick cock.

I bend to suckle her perky nipple, sending more spirals of pleasure through her body. My cock pummels in and out of her hard and fast. I don't hold back, even when she squeaks with ecstasy and her pussy gushes hot, slippery honey all over my member. I grope her tits, lewdly feeling her up while I pound into her. She feels so fucking good, so tight and twinging around my thickness. I slide out and back in again, pumping my hips faster and harder by the second.

"You're going to remember this," I grunt. "Your body won't let you forget how good I make you feel."

Hartley is beyond words by now. Her gorgeous face is twisted in ecstasy, her body almost limp as she gives me total control. I reach down to massage her clit with two fingers while I fuck her, and before long, she's writhing again with another orgasm.

"Oh my god, oh my god," she pants.

"*Da, printsessa,*" I growl, my accent coming out stronger now as I lose control.

"It feels—so good," she breathes. "I want you to—to—"

I cover her mouth with one hand and watch her eyes go from fear to satisfaction when I rut into her harder than before. My pace quickens, getting irregular as tension builds in my core. I love the feeling of Hartley's breath warm on my palm, the sight of her tits bouncing with every thrust of my hips. Finally, it becomes too much.

With one deep growl of pleasure, my cock spurts hot seed deep inside her warm cunt. She's still clenching around me, her pussy tingling with the aftershocks of her own climaxes. I pump in and out a few more times, making sure to empty every last drop inside her. I move my hand from her mouth and she sucks in a deep breath, her cheeks going pink. I withdraw from her and she whimpers, like she misses my cock already.

I bring her a fluffy, warm towel from the ensuite bathroom. I gingerly untie her wrists, dab her down, kiss her on the lips. I stroke her hair and nuzzle so close to her ear it makes her squirm. I hear her utter one phrase, soft and sweet.

"Did I do good?"

I climb into bed beside her and drape my arms around her naked body. I lean in and whisper in her ear, "You were a very good little slut."

She seems content with that answer, not to mention overwhelmed with exhaustion. It's only a few minutes of holding her before her blue eyes roll shut. Her breaths come slow and rhythmic, and I know she's asleep. I watch the moonlight dance across her face as the minutes tick toward early morning. This girl has no idea of the web she's wandered into. She's caught in my grasp now, and I have no intention of letting her go so easily. I have plans for her.

I let myself drift to sleep, secure in the knowledge that Hartley won't escape me. She's too tired to move, her clothes are downstairs in the foyer, and she won't be able to get up without my noticing. Besides, the downstairs front door is locked—from the inside and the outside. Only I know the sequence. As much as this girl might believe this is a regular one-night stand, she couldn't be more wrong. There is nothing regular about me, about us.

But when I wake up hours later, I'm surprised to find myself alone in bed. I get up immediately and begin looking around for Hartley. She isn't in the bathroom, nor do I find her downstairs. Her clothes are still on the floor of the foyer, and the security system is glowing green, just like last night. Indicating that nobody has even attempted the code since then.

When I go back upstairs, I see that her panties and bra are still on the bedroom floor. Her shoes, however, are missing. On a hunch, I open the door to my walk-in closet. There, on the rack, I see a discrepancy. I organize my clothing, as well as all my belongings, in a very specific way. I know immediately what's missing: a pair of black athletic shorts and a large white t-shirt.

I check the window. I can't help but smile wryly to myself when I notice the tiniest crack between the window and the sill. I wrench the window open and look down.

"Well, that is unexpected," I murmur

I stand there, bemused at the realization that Hartley has managed to slip out of my embrace, steal my clothes, pry the window open, and climb down three flights of the fire escape. All without waking me, and all in three-inch heels.

If anything, her clever escape only further ignites that desire inside me. She impressed me last night, but now I am fully obsessed. I'm hardly even disappointed to have lost her. Because now, I have a new goal: to find her again. And this time, I will make sure she cannot get away.

This time, she will be *mine*.

CHAPTER 4

HARTLEY

I wrap my fluffy orange scarf a little tighter around my neck. I brace for the chilly wind as I step out of the brick building. It's a Monday in late October, and I'm just leaving campus after a full morning of classes. I look both ways before I cross the road to the sidewalk running alongside St. James Park. A cool breeze ruffles my hair, making the ends flutter around my shoulders. I adjust the strap of my school satchel slung over my shoulder and take my phone out of the side pocket. The time reads half past noon, and my stomach gives me a little warning growl. I haven't had anything substantial to eat or drink since early this morning.

As is my usual Monday routine, I rose before the sun this morning to fit in a workout before my first class. Sure, I have time in the afternoons to do that, but I've always been an early riser anyway. I love the calm and stillness of early morning, before all of New York City has time to wake up. It feels peaceful, looking out the one tiny window in my kitchen to see the first glow of sunrise peeking out behind the Bronx skyline. The streets are quieter then, before the commuters and the college students clog the veins of the city. I always like to start my day with a little exercise. It gets my heart rate up, wakes my brain up, and gives me a little punch of adrenaline to propel me forward. At first, I needed those endorphins just to get myself out the front door and down the five flights of stairs to the street. Now, it's just a habit.

In the past month or so, I've even become brave enough to go for short jogs around my neighborhood around dawn. For a long time, I wouldn't dare put myself in that situation: tight, skimpy running clothes combined with nearly empty streets and nobody to call for help if something did happen? No, thank you. I've been too cautious with my new identity to risk it, until recently.

I guess enough time has passed that I'm starting to feel at home here. It's not just my hidey hole in the city, it's my stomping grounds now. I know there are technically much 'nicer' parts of the city, but this is my neighborhood, and I've grown to love the rough edges of the Bronx. It's noisy. It's busy. It's packed with strangers, any of whom could be an enemy. But over time, you get used to your surroundings, no matter what they are. Even my tiny studio apartment feels like an oasis to me now, a safe haven from the rest of the world. My home is essentially just one large room with a kitchenette and a tiny bathroom. The only natural light comes in through that teeny kitchen window at a certain time of day. The walls are thin, and I can hear not only my downstairs neighbors but the people in the building next door all day and night. This close to campus, I'm surrounded by my fellow classmates, most of whom are more focused on partying than finishing a degree. The weekends are loud and sloppy, and I've seen a lot of petty, tipsy drama unfold right on the street outside my building.

However, nothing bad has happened to me.

Yet, I remind myself.

I follow my routine. I keep to myself. I go to class, I come home, I do my homework, I exercise. Sometimes when I'm feeling especially down, I pick myself up with an elaborate home-cooked meal. I find ways to pass the time, and my old wounds hardly ache anymore. As the days go by, it feels more and more like progress. Like my cobbled-together new life is real. It may not always be pretty, but it's my little bubble. And every day I go through my routine without issue, my bubble gets a tiny bit bigger.

By the playground, a trio of moms sit on a bench watching their assorted toddlers climb, slide, and swing. The moms joke around and sip coffee out of thermoses. I wonder what their lives are like, who they go home to, if they're happy. I smile at a group of teenagers goofing around on the tennis court. They're too young to be college students, most likely a bunch of latchkey kids who have been playing in this park since they were children. An elderly couple walks past me hand-in-hand, the man looking sweetly into the face of his wife as she concentrates on using her cane. I can feel the love between them just from one glance. It warms my heart to see all these people living their lives, being happy and unafraid.

I want that someday.

As I step out the other side of St. James Park, that warm feeling starts to fade. I keep heading in the direction of my apartment, maybe a ten-minute walk away. I try to ignore the growing sense of unease in my body. The hairs on the back of my neck stand up. A shiver runs down my spine. I glance around, trying to seem casual while I check my surroundings. There are people everywhere, of course. Pedestrians on the sidewalk, tons of traffic in the street. I scan every face, my heart starting to beat faster. I can't shake the sensation that someone is watching me. Following me. But when I look around, nobody seems focused on me.

I'm being paranoid.

After everything and everyone I've run away from, it makes sense. I can't remember when I was first taught how to pick up on the fact that someone's following me, but it was definitely before I learned addition and subtraction.

And the first rule is to trust my gut.

If there *is* someone following me, the last thing I want is to lead them right to my home address. I decide I'll head to my favorite local coffee shop, a little hole-in-the-wall where the baristas recognize me. If nothing else, it will be a nice break to sit down and sip a delicious brown sugar latte. I can even do some reading for class while I'm there. It's just a regular Monday, but why not treat myself?

Plus, it feels safer to go someplace surrounded by other people. Nothing crazy is going to happen to me in the middle of a bustling coffee shop. So I make my way the two blocks down to Creston Cafe, all the while trying to ignore the pervasive sense of being tailed. I glance behind myself several times on the walk, but every time, it feels like someone slips out of my line of vision just before I turn to look. Each empty glance makes me more uneasy instead of calming my nerves, so the jingling bells above the cafe door are a truly welcoming sound.

I join the short queue of patrons at the counter, giving a wave to my favorite barista. She grins and waves back from beside the espresso machine. The cafe is pleasantly busy, with nearly all the tables full. There's a low hum of conversation and laughter layered over the soft, calming muzak. They have Halloween decor strung up about the place, with tiny pumpkins perched on each table, and a fake spiderweb hung from the ceiling. I breathe in the slightly spicy, comforting scent of freshly-ground coffee and feel a little calmer as I approach the counter.

The barista, a girl about my age with blue hair and a nose ring, gives me a big smile.

"Hey there, Maggie! Good to see you again," she greets me brightly.

"Hi, good to see you, too. Love the Halloween decorations," I tell her.

"Thanks! It's finally starting to feel like autumn out there," she remarks. "So, are you having the usual?"

"Yes, please," I reply, reaching for the cash in my satchel pocket.

"You got it. One brown sugar latte with two-percent milk," she says, typing it into the cash register. She takes my money and begins to write my name on a coffee cup. She glances up, looking thoughtful.

"Maggie… so, is that short for Margaret or Mary?" she asks, clearly just making conversation. But her question makes me instantly freeze up. I feel my cheeks flushing pink as I struggle to find a response.

Guilt hangs heavy in my heart. I should know what 'Maggie' is short for. But I don't, and the opportunity to find out disappeared a long time ago. Just like she did. Along with any semblance of love and security I ever felt.

"Uhh, oh, I'm not sure. I-I think it's a family name," I lie quickly.

In a way, it *is* a family name. But not the kind of family you'd expect. And it's certainly not the name I was given at birth. I keep that, just like everything else about the way I grew up, a secret. It was hard at first, to learn how to answer to someone else's name. To forget who I was in order to become who I am now.

But my family didn't leave me with a lot of choices.

"Well, it's a nice name either way," answers the barista with a wink. "Enjoy your latte!"

"Thank you," I tell her, and slide down to grab my piping-hot coffee. I manage to find a seat by the entrance, only a couple feet from where the queue starts. I sit down and take out one of my textbooks to look over while I sip my drink.

That old version of myself would be shocked at my new life. Growing up, my father always told me horror stories about the dangers of the big city. He taught me to fear the outside world. We kept to ourselves. I learned to hide, to never trust anyone but family. As I grew older and I figured things out, I learned I couldn't trust them either.

So, I have to be Maggie now. It's a small price to pay for a taste of freedom.

I haven't given anyone my real name since three months ago, when I met that mysterious, sexy stranger at the Velvet Kiss Lounge. That was a slip-up on my part. I don't know how he did it, but that man seduced me into giving up control. I let him take the reins, and put my fragile new identity at risk.

That's why I climbed out his window.

I *have* to be the one in control.

I can't allow any mistakes.

Who knows what my family would do if they found me now?

Sure, he probably woke up to find me gone, put two and two together, and now thinks I'm absolutely insane. I mean, what kind of girl steals your clothes and climbs down the fire escape instead of simply waiting until morning or asking for cab fare home? I panicked a little, but what else could I do? Let him think we were a genuine item and spread my real name around town?

And if I gave in to temptation, let romance blossom between us—when would he ask to meet my parents?

No. I can't go down that path. I have a plan: get my culinary arts degree, find a job in the back of some fancy restaurant, and lie low for the rest of my life. If that means cutting off the opportunity for lust and romance in the process, then so be it. A lonely life, but at least it's mine. And when it all gets to be too much, at least I have the memories of that one-night-stand to warm me up.

For once, I gave up control, and I felt… safe.

I had never felt safe growing up.

And I hadn't felt safe since I fled down his fire escape.

But in his arms, under his dominant command, I had learned what safety could feel like.

My thoughts keep drifting back to him as I try to read my book, and my anxiety begins to slowly ebb away. The sweet coffee chases the autumn chill from my bones, and I relax into the chair as I become more engrossed in the novel. An hour or so passes, and I turn to look out the window to check if anyone was watching me.

To my surprise, the room tilts on its axis. My stomach lurches. I feel dizzy, blinking rapidly to try and focus my eyes. My body feels tingly and loose. I take a sip of my latte, now starting to get cold. It tastes fine, but a wave of nausea passes over me. I feel like I've just taken my seventh shot of the evening rather than a sip of coffee. I feel drunk.

"Whoa," I murmur weakly.

Maybe my workout this morning wore me out more than I even expected. All at once, I decide I have to get out of here. If I'm coming down with some kind of bug, I need to be at home. Safe and alone.

My vision is blurry as I slowly stand up, scoop my stuff into my satchel, and wobble out the door onto the street. I stumble and shiver in the cold afternoon air. I can hardly tell up from down. I wobble from one side of the pavement to the other, bumping into the occasional pedestrian with a slurred, "Sorry."

This isn't right.

This isn't a cold.

I turn to look back at the coffee shop, spinning as I try to make my limbs move. I should go back in. I should be around people, people who know me. The barista should still be there, I could tell her to call someone.

Who?

The cops?

My fake ID is good, but I'm not exactly looking to test and see *how* good it is.

I feel like I could crumple to the asphalt any second now. My building is so close, just a block away, and then I could hide. I turn away from the coffee shop, and find myself taking a familiar shortcut through a dim alleyway. I had taken it dozens of times, but now it feels so quiet, so empty. The world expands and contracts in on itself, and I have to push my palm to one of the buildings for support.

"What is happening to me?" I hear myself whisper.

It looks so dark outside, too dark for the afternoon. I realize it's my eyes closing. My field of vision shrinks down further and further. Distantly, I begin to make out the sound of soft footsteps getting closer and closer behind me.

"No. No," I breathe. My knees buckle underneath me.

The world mutes down to a pinprick of light. Darkness comes choking in. I gasp at the sudden pressure of strong arms wrapping around me, and everything turns black.

CHAPTER 5

ZAKHAR

She's mine again.

Caught in my snare like a perfect little white rabbit.

My eyes narrow as I lean forward, focusing on the multiple computer screens in front of me. It's dark in this room except for the unearthly bluish glow of the monitors and a single lightbulb dangling overhead. It's not even a real room, just a walk-in closet reconfigured in the shape of a security office. There are always changes to be made when the Bratva acquire a new piece of property.

From the outside, the building looks like any other in Brooklyn. A five-story apartment building with a red brick facade and wrought-iron balconies on the third and fifth floors. Each floor of the building is occupied with an active renter on the lease, including this top-level apartment. But instead of random strangers who may or may not object to the illicit activities being run out of their building, it's fully populated with mafia plants.

There are a few low-ranking members, the kind of

strong, silent men who do as they're told without question. They are runners, nearly pawns for the organization. And then there are some civilians who have lived in this neighborhood for decades. They are the backbone of Brighton Beach: Russian-Americans who regard the Bratva as a necessary evil… or even just necessary. They enjoy the relative protection of living within our stomping grounds in exchange for helping keep our secrets. They just want a quiet, safe place to maintain their traditions from the motherland, and we are happy to provide it. After all, we are on the same side, and we've learned that an integrated approach works best. If you want to truly control a place, you have to blend in. Only once you've wormed your tendrils into every dark corner can you call it yours.

Besides, there's no better camouflage for crime than a peaceful community. No one would suspect that this building, right down the street from an in-home daycare and a quaint Russian convenience store, has played host to captors and captives alike.

On the inside, though, this apartment is more specifically outfitted for my line of work. In this former walk-in closet, the racks and hangers have been removed to make space for three computer screens on a hefty industrial desk. I sit in a cushy, black armchair with a swivel, my hand resting on the mouse pad of the main computer. With one click, I can zoom in on any of the displays in front of me. The cameras run day and night, with a backup generator to maintain their perfect, consistent service.

In addition, the original, mounted full-length mirror in here was traded out for a panel of one-way glass to my right, along the wall shared with the ensuite bathroom. By just glancing over, I have a window into the bathroom through the mirror over the sink. It just so happens to have a full view of the entire bathroom—toilet, shower, and tub. So, even if my little captive princess tries to hide from me in there, I can still find her. The girl is clever enough to be trouble, which I like. But it does mean she requires a little extra effort to contain.

Isn't that the way it goes, though?

Anything worth having is worth fighting for.

If my steamy memory of our first tryst is any indication, this girl is *definitely* worth having. And worth keeping all to myself, if I can help it.

At least for the time being.

I have waited and watched from afar for long enough. Now that she's under my thumb, I intend to take my time. To really relish every look, every touch, every command I force her to obey. I remember how good she was before—how she submitted to my control almost immediately. Like she understood exactly what to do.

I knew at that moment I had found someone truly special.

A woman who would obey me, but could also keep up with me.

I had begun to think such a companion couldn't exist. My life is too cold, too cruel. My work is too violent. I have too much responsibility. And yet, something about the girl tells me she could be the one to shoulder some of that burden with me.

For three long months, I have allowed myself to have fantasies of a forbidden nature for a man like me.

Fantasies of a future with her.

But first, I have to be sure.

I could have taken her much sooner. As bustling as the

city is, I know New York City like the back of my hand by
now. I know the back roads. I know the secret places. If I
want to track someone down, I'll do it. Fast. Whether or
not they give me their real name.

"Hartley," I murmur to myself.

The name still tastes so good on my tongue. It feels
real. When she gave it to me, I detected no dishonesty. But
when I searched for her by name, I found dead ends over
and over again. So many dead ends, in fact, that I assume
she was trying to *keep* it dead. That was confirmed for me
when I discovered her in the Bronx, telling people her
name is Maggie. That's the name on the collegiate letters
coming to her building. And it was the name scrawled on
her coffee cup in black marker.

It was the first month when I found her. The second
month, I nailed down her schedule. I knew her classes, her
breaks, her morning routine, even the little things she did
to mix it up. Lucky for me, Hartley is a creature of habit.
Once I figured out the few locations she frequented, it was
easy to watch her. I could almost be disappointed that she
never went back to the Velvet Kiss, except she never went
to any other bars either. In all the time I watched her, I
never saw her so much as glance at another man, and I
have to admit, it stoked my fires even hotter to know that I
was something special to her.

But by the third month, simply following her was not
enough. I needed to possess her, to keep her locked up like
a precious object. Just for me. I've waited so long to claim
her again. I dreamed up a thousand ways to capture her.

Drugging her coffee was risky. Something out of character for me. I'd beaten men for drugging women before,
but we all rationalize the dark things we do as justifiable.

Truth is, I was obsessed. I needed to have her. Simple as that.

I had watched her sip the drugged coffee, unaware. I saw her stand up, wobbly and confused, and gather her things to leave. I followed her as she stumbled down the sidewalk in a daze. It was strange to feel a single, sharp pang of worry for her. I have used this method before, and will probably do it again. I've committed far fouler sins in my line of work than drugging Hartley.

But never for this purpose.

And that voice in the back of my head that wondered if she would be okay was… new. I don't enjoy seeing her in distress; at least, not *that* kind. The fear in her mind, the weakness in her body.

I tracked her into that dim alleyway as she slowed down and began to lose consciousness, like a wolf tailing a wounded doe. I swept over her as her pretty eyes rolled back in her head. I scooped her into my arms and silently carried her a block away to my car. If you move with enough purpose, you can get away with anything in this dirty city. I tipped her into the backseat of my car and came straight here to the Brighton Beach safehouse.

I look at her on the monitors. Three different angles of Hartley lying flat on the bed with a sophisticated latched blindfold over her eyes and her kissable lips ever so slightly parted. If not for her chest gently rising and falling, she would look like the most beautiful corpse entombed in a generic bedroom. It's sparsely furnished with just a four-post bed, a dresser affixed to the wall so that she can't move it in front of the door, and a large map of Siberia hung up over the spot where a window once overlooked the alley below. Now, the window has been bricked in. Just another wall of Hartley's holding cell. No chance of her fleeing down a fire escape this time.

She's just lying there in her white sweater and jeans, a sleeping beauty on a countdown for the drugs to wear off. I confiscated her brown jacket, boots, socks, and orange scarf, but I stopped short of stripping her nude. It will be frightening enough for her to wake up to find her wrists and ankles bound and her vision totally obscured. The least I can do is give her an ounce of dignity for her suffering.

I wonder how long it will take her to come back to reality, and after that, how long before she escapes her bindings? I have intentionally restrained her in a way that she could unravel with a little patience and persistence. I have to test her.

I see the first sign of consciousness: her left pinky finger twitches.

"It begins," I growl, preparing to watch the show. But before I can settle in, my phone screen lights up with a message. It's from a blocked number, with just one word.

Here.

I step out of the security room and almost immediately bump into a tall man with dark blond hair and green eyes, dressed in all black. He's an Avtoritet, but he's also my friend. We've known each other for years. Even our mothers play cards together.

Still, I outrank him, and I need to get rid of him quickly.

"Arseny," I greet him with a handshake. "You're early."

My friend nods. "*Izvinee.* Leon is requesting the key for the Lancaster Street safehouse. Apparently, they have a lot of goods to hold until the ferry tomorrow."

I fish the key out of my pocket and hand it to him, but he looks distracted. He peers over my shoulder at the monitors and frowns. "Is that a girl?" he asks.

"Good observation," I remark. He doesn't laugh.

"I didn't realize we have a captive here. Does the Pakhan know about this one?" he questions in a lower voice.

"I'm the Obshchak," I answer plainly. "Everything I do is cleared by the Pakhan."

It's not quite the truth. Not everything I do is cleared ahead of time. Like this captive. Looking into his eyes, Arseny knows I'm lying. We've been friends for too long, and he can detect the dishonesty in my words even when most people have no idea. But he also knows I outrank him. It's not a fact I bring up often, mostly because it goes unspoken. He understands his place in the organization and so do I, regardless of our shared background. He looks at Hartley, then back to me. I can tell he wants to speak up. Maybe to warn me about the dangers of bringing outsiders into our world or utilizing mafia property for my own personal use. But instead, he swallows his questions.

"Well, I shouldn't keep Leon waiting," he says finally.

"No. You shouldn't," I agree. "He's not a patient man."

He pockets the safehouse key and turns to leave down the hallway. Just as the elevator door is closing, he says, "Be careful, Zak."

I give him a solid nod before the doors shut and he disappears. With his warning still fresh in my mind, I return to the security room. I smile to myself when I see Hartley's perfect body wiggling around. She's waking up and realizing the predicament she's in. There's no audio in the security footage, and the walls of her cell are insulated to keep sounds in, but I can imagine her whimpering. Hyperventilating. Maybe calling for help.

But she isn't totally helpless on her own. In fact, despite her weakened state and her panicked mind, she manages to slowly undo her ankle bindings. She stands up on wobbly feet and paces blindly in her cell, picking at her wrist bindings with the tips of her fingernails. Her mouth is open now, shaping into words I can't hear, but I can see.

Help me. Somebody, please help me.

Her hands move to the back of her head, her hands shaking violently as she tries to unlace the blindfold, which is too securely fastened to slip right off. She fidgets with the blindfold for a few moments, then suddenly stops and lets her arms drop to her sides. I furrow my brow, watching her with interest. She's wiggled free of her bindings, yet she won't remove the blindfold. It's more elegantly designed than a basic fabric tie-around, but it's not impossible, or even that difficult. Especially for an intelligent, resourceful girl like Hartley.

She's not even trying.

Instead, Hartley feels around for the bed and sinks down on the edge of it. She sits still, just breathing. Like she's waiting for something.

Like she's waiting for *me*.

CHAPTER 6

HARTLEY

"Help. Help me," I hear somebody calling out weakly. "Please, somebody."

The voice sounds muffled and hoarse, like someone talking with a sore throat and a pillow over their face. It takes me a good minute or so for it to dawn on me that it's my own voice I'm hearing. My own throat that sounds so scratchy, my own lips struggling to form the words. That in itself is frustrating to me. It feels like my brain is working at half capacity, as though parts of me are still trying to wake up from a deep sleep. My stomach lurches and nausea washes over me.

"Ugh," I mumble, wrapping my arms over my stomach and folding over with my forehead almost on my knees.

This simple tilt forward sends my disoriented brain into sparks and crackles, like the popping of lights behind the eyes right before you pass out. My head aches deep inside, and I wonder what the hell happened to me. Did someone attack me with a blow to the head? How much time has passed? Do I have a concussion?

My fingernails are all chipped and rough from the several minutes I spent picking frantically at my ankle and wrist bindings. They are made of simple but incredibly robust rope material, fitted into knots that took all my wobbly concentration to unravel. I'm not much of an outdoorsy girl, but I'm pretty sure it's the same kind of rope hikers use to climb mountains.

And my brain won't let me forget that it's the same kind of rope every TV show serial killer keeps in the secret compartment of his car for on-the-go kidnapping. I swallow hard, hoping that's not the kind of person I'm dealing with here. But it tracks, doesn't it? The last thing I remember before that is drinking my coffee, stumbling down the street, and fainting in the alley before somebody dragged me off to this mysterious place. Who would do that but some kind of predatory monster?

Yet, the bindings on my ankles and wrists were manageable to untie. Even in my weakened, panicked state, I'm able to wriggle free with some persistence. How could my captor be skilled enough to kidnap me right off the street in my own neighborhood and deposit me here, but not skilled enough to construct secure knots? It seems like Kidnapping 101-level stuff: tying the right knots to properly contain your captive. Something tells me I'm not dealing with a rookie, though. Which means that he made my wrist and ankle bindings flimsy on purpose.

But what purpose? To test me? To fuck with my head?

On the other hand, the blindfold obscuring my eyes is tight around my face, with some kind of intricate lacing at the back. It's made of a different, more slippery material. My fingers are too numb, my hands too shaky to remove the blindfold right now. Besides, I know better than to just expose myself like that. I've watched enough true crime documentaries to realize how dangerous it is to see your captor's face. He could've put a weak blindfold on me to match the ineffective rope ties, but he didn't. That means something. Up until now, he's been operating in secrecy. I don't know who he is, so I can't identify him. I can't be a witness.

But if I were to see his face, he might have to eliminate me.

So I let my arms drop to my sides. I fall back against the bed, feeling the edge of the mattress sink a little underneath me. I begin to feel around slowly. I touch my own body and I'm relieved to find that I'm still wearing my jeans and sweater. I realize with a jolt, though, that this means my captive took off my shoes, boots, scarf, and jacket. I shiver. Goosebumps pop up on my skin as I think about some strange man touching my unconscious body. Removing articles of clothing, taking his time while I'm knocked out.

Again, if he had me in such a vulnerable position, why did he leave me any clothes at all? Perhaps it's a bleak way to look at the world, but I would expect much worse from a man in full, unabated control of a woman's limp body. He could have stripped me nude. He could have hurt me badly. But despite the ache in my head and my overall discomfort, I don't feel wounded.

The more I try to figure him out, the more confused I get. I start to stand up again, to begin feeling my way around the room to get my bearings. But then I hear the first outside noise so far—beyond my shallow breathing, I hear the soft rhythmic thumping of footsteps. They're somehow slow and soft but heavy at the same time, like a large person moving lightly. My heart races as the footsteps get louder. He's coming closer and closer.

Finally, the steps stop not far from me. Close enough that I can smell a new scent, something that wasn't there before. It's a combination of a man's natural musk and some kind of fancy cologne. It makes my mouth water instantly. With my eyes covered, my sense of smell feels heightened. Memories come flooding back to me in little flashes of vivid color and sensation. Crimson lighting, body heat, and that delicious, enticing cologne washing over me. I soak in his scent, in his closeness, in my mingled fear and curiosity.

The tension is palpable. I feel his eyes on me. I'm waiting for him to make his next move.

"You're awake," comes a deep, gruff voice from several feet away.

I perk up, facing the sound. His voice is intensely familiar.

I stammer, "Wh-what happened to me? Where am I?"

"You took a stumble. Now you're here," he answers cryptically.

"Please, I don't want any trouble," I tell him.

"And yet it seems to follow you," he says.

"No, no. This must be a mistake," I insist.

I feel the air around me shift. He's moving closer. I'm hit with another whiff of that cologne. Despite my fear, I find myself leaning toward him, as though there's some mystical magnetic force pulling me to my captor. My heart is thumping so hard, it aches. Every cell in my body is on fire, burning hotter with every step closer he takes. I feel a large, calloused hand touch my cheek. I gasp in surprise and jump back a little at first, but then I can't help but push into the warmth of his palm.

"I don't make mistakes," the man growls.

The feeling of his hand on my cheek elicits another muddled flash of memory. A dark bedroom. Hands roving up and down my body. My knees on the floor.

I can hear my own voice asking, *"Who are you?"*

And the answer: *"I am your master."*

The reality of my situation crashes into me like a freight train. I do know this man, or at least he knows me. That cologne, that warm touch, that husky voice—I recognize it all. He is the man who has infiltrated all my filthiest, steamiest dreams. He's the one who shook me out of my routine, who made me forget who I am.

He's the man I've been trying so hard to forget about for the past three months.

"It's you," I breathe. "From the Velvet Kiss Lounge."

"Clever girl. I knew it would come to you," he murmurs.

"Why are you doing this?" I ask him. My lip trembles, but I try to remain calm.

He doesn't answer, but his hand slides up the side of my face and smooths back through my hair. As fearful as I am, my body still responds to his touch. I'm tingling from head to toe. With my eyes covered, it's like every physical sensation is intensified. His caress is borderline orgasmic. But it's also intoxicating. It's misleading. This man is temptation himself, and I was a fool to let him corrupt me, because I've been desperately aching for him ever since.

Dancing with him was a slip-up. Going home with him was a mistake. And telling him my real name could've cost me everything—my safety, my identity, my hard-won freedom. It took all my strength to run away from my past and start fresh in the Bronx. It took years of building up courage and planning the details of my escape. I left home and all that I had known, trading it for a slim chance of making it on my own. I got myself into culinary school under my new identity. I even managed to score a scholarship. I was building a life—a false one, but a life nonetheless. I didn't allow anything to distract me from my goals. No man could tear me away from my studies or make me waver in my newfound freedom.

Not until I met *him* at the Velvet Kiss. One touch of his magic hands, and I threw caution to the wind. All my hard work could have been ruined in one undeniably steamy hookup.

And what does it say about me that I so eagerly fell into his trap? After the things I've been through, I was sure I'd never let a man control me again. I would be the sole master of my own fate. But he makes me question what it means to be free. If giving up my agency to this man feels so damn good, what does that make me? Weak? Broken? Perverse?

He pulls his hand back, and I feel the loss like an open wound. I lean toward him, straining for a morsel of his attention. I should be afraid. I *am* afraid. But my desire is more insistent than my fear. He snaps his finger.

"On your knees," he commands roughly. "Hands behind your back."

Like clockwork, I slide off the edge of the bed and kneel down. My knees touch the cold, hard floor. I put my arms behind my back and tilt up to him, even though I can't see. I hear him step back from me.

"Put your forehead to the floor. Submit to me," he

orders.

"Okay, okay," I whisper fervently as I rush to follow his instruction. I lean over, arms still behind my back, until my forehead touches the cold tile. He makes me stay like this a few moments before he gives his next command.

"Kneel for me. Open your mouth."

I lift back up and part my lips. My heart races. I wonder what's to come next. I'm desperate for his touch, for his taste. And at the same time, I'm disgusted with myself for wanting him so badly. What kind of woman craves the affection of a cruel master?

It strikes me once again that I hardly know this man. I don't know his name. In fact, with this blindfold on, I start to question whether he's the man from the club at all. Every instinct in my body tells me that it's really him, but I could be wrong. I thought I was smart enough to take care of myself, too, and apparently, I was wrong about that.

Suddenly, I'm questioning everything. As his hand slips down to my throat and his long fingers slowly wrap around my neck, I choke out the one strange word that has been rattling around in my head for three months.

"Nyet!" I blurt out.

I freeze up. If it's him, he'll understand. If it's not him… my outburst will mean nothing.

"You remember," he growls in approval. "Very good."

To my surprise, his hand loosens from my neck. He strokes my hair softly. I push up into his hand, sighing with pleasure. Relief floods over me. I should still be afraid, but I'm mostly just content to bask in his presence. As long as he's touching me, there's nowhere else I could be. I'm almost ashamed of how much I crave his affection.

When he pulls away, I let out a soft whimper. "No. No, please stay," I mutter.

"Be good, Hartley," he replies in that familiar gruff voice.

I hear him walk off, and then a door creaks shut. I hear the lock engage.

All the tingling hope in my body fades away, and I crumple to the floor. Tears burn in my eyes and soak the blindfold. I reach back to start feverishly unlacing it. I have to see where he went. I have to figure out how to get back to him. But when I finally get the blindfold off and my eyes adjust to the light, all I see is a generic bedroom with the only door shut and locked. On unsteady legs I wobble to the door and press against it, desperately listening for any sign of him. But I hear only silence and my own labored breathing.

I sink down to the floor, my back against the door. Tears roll down my cheeks. Even though I ran away from him three months ago, all I want is for him to come back and touch me again. I thought I was okay on my own. But I understand now—that night we spent together changed me. He's given me a taste, and now I'm hooked.

How long will he leave me waiting this time?

CHAPTER 7

ZAKHAR

I t's difficult to walk away from her.

I never expected it to feel this way, as though I'm abandoning my post by leaving her behind. Usually, my ambition and loyalty lie with only one entity: the organization. As long as I follow my orders and stick to my missions, I enjoy a near-constant sense of satisfaction. I'm good at my line of work. For years, I have had no real distractions from that work. But now, I have to admit that there is something else tugging at my attention, someone new for me to protect. Hartley is not my usual captive.

Most of my interpersonal dealings involve other members of the mafia, generally men. Even in the rare case when a woman is involved, my focus never wavers. Not until now.

Because Hartley is special, and she fascinates me.

Hearing her sweet, soft voice cry out that safeword surprised me. She remembered it after all this time, and was daring enough to use it. I could feel the desire in her voice, underneath the fear. She has every reason to recoil from me. I am her captor. I could do whatever I want with her, and I'm sure she knows that. And yet, when I was in the bedroom with her, she didn't try to hide. She didn't pull away. In fact, she leaned toward me.

Hartley wants this as badly as I do, even if she's confused as to why. She's not used to submitting to a man this way and liking it. Loving it, even. She wants to resist —that's the rebel inside of her. I bet she's used to saying no. But not to me. And it drives her wild.

When I look at her, I see potential. She has exactly the kind of spark I've been searching for all these years of lonely service. I enjoy a lot of power in my position. A fair amount of freedom, too. But one thing I've had to give up is any hope of having a lifelong companion. It's damn near impossible to find a woman clever and resourceful enough to survive in my world. Even if I do, there's still the issue that she's a distraction from my work, a liability to the Bratva, and yet another innocent soul I must protect from our enemies that lurk in the shadows.

The most painful aspect that keeps me from allowing true love into my life is the understanding that, in order to be mine, a woman must give up her old ways for a strange, dangerous new path beside me. That kind of sacrifice is too great. I cannot demand that a woman with a completely normal background and a normal life turn away from everything she's ever known to run wild with me. I am a powerful man. I've worked hard to rise through the ranks, to establish my position near the top. But that doesn't mark me safe from the dangers I must face every day. I'm used to it, but I could never ask a woman to accept the same.

Still, I'm a man with needs. I haven't remained

completely celibate all these long years. Far from it—I can land just about any woman I meet. When I walk into a place like the Velvet Kiss Lounge, my choices are laid out for me like a lineup. I follow my lust to its inevitable destination, and I have never been rejected once. I know I'm a good-looking man, but it's more than that. Women respond to the dominant in me, even if they don't get it. For one night and with a false name, I use them to release my pent-up sensual energy. But it never goes beyond one night. By morning, I've disappeared, never to return again.

She doesn't have my name, and I make it a point to not ask for hers. It's cleaner that way. If we don't know each other's names, there's no temptation to look her up or vice versa. Besides, none of these women have ever come close to truly fulfilling my needs in the bedroom. They can try, but they can't match my requirements. I assumed nobody could.

Until Hartley came falling into my lap. I have no choice but to be obsessed with her. She knows how to serve, how to obey. It comes naturally to her. If she was only so submissive now as a captive at my mercy, perhaps I wouldn't think twice. After all, it's easy to relinquish control when you so clearly have none to begin with. But her submission to me first came under no threat at all, three months ago in the relative safety of my loft apartment. Under no duress. With no expectations beyond a night of shared pleasure. That shows me her obedience is something innate to her but hidden, something only I can coax out of her.

On top of her bedroom performance, she also stands out as being cleverer than the average girl. She is a fast learner. She thinks of her feet. Even after a night of drinking and rough sex, she had the wherewithal to steal my clothes and get away down the fire escape. How she managed to do it without waking me is still a mystery. My vigilance makes me an extremely light sleeper—you never know who will try to stab you while you're down. And yet, this supposedly 'normal' young woman slinks away into the night, almost without a trace.

Then, she easily shed her ankle and wrist bindings. She was also thoughtful enough to remember that safeword and pull it out in context. She remembered it, so I know for certain that our night of passion impacted her as much as it did me. She's tried to move on, but Hartley just can't forget about me, about how I made her feel that night. I bet she's been fantasizing about our tryst ever since. She's insanely beautiful. She takes good care of her body—giving her the strength to keep up with me in and out of the bedroom.

Despite my growing fascination with this pretty play-thing, I drag myself away to carry out work orders for the day. It's not even dawn when I lock up the safehouse and quietly leave in my black sedan. I glance back at the building in my overhead mirror, looking at the bricked-over spot where the fifth-floor bedroom window would be. I think about Hartley just on the other side. I'm confident she can't escape; the safehouse is specifically outfitted to contain captives. And that's a good thing, because I can't afford to lose her. Not only because I'm obsessed with making her mine, but because she would be a major liability to the mafia. She could rat out the safehouse location or describe me to the authorities. That would put my brethren in jeopardy, of course, but it would also make her a target. Someone to be eliminated for the sake of the Bratva.

And then there's my sneaking suspicion that she's already a target. That girl is running from something—otherwise, why the fake identity of 'Maggie'? Still, at least as long as she's in my grasp, I know she is safe.

My first mission for the day brings me all the way out to Long Island. My work as second in command to the Pakhan means keeping the Avtoritets in line. I have to make sure their operations run smoothly, that they remain focused and loyal. I received word in the middle of the night that there was an altercation at a mafia-run gas station out on a back road near East Quogue, along the southern coast of Long Island. It's a nearly three-hour drive from the safehouse in Brighton Beach. It's still dark outside when I leave, and I'm pleased to find the roads somewhat empty this time of morning. By the time I pull up to the gas station, the sun is merely a pale glow on the horizon.

The gas station is an unassuming cinder block building with two modest fuel pumps out front, which are old enough to look like antiques. The lot is only dimly lit by one weak, fluttering streetlight. The gas station has the usual signs in English indicating fuel prices and the like, but there are also Russian-language flyers and signs on the windows. I park on the darkened side of the building and follow along the shadows to the entrance. There's a CLOSED sign on the door, but it opens right up when I push through.

Inside, it looks perfectly normal. It's clean and every shelf is fully stocked with basic necessities as well as some specialty Russian treats. Over the intercom, a vaguely familiar Russian pop song from decades ago plays softly. It's dim in here, except for the fluorescent panel over the counter, illuminating the old woman seated there. She looks up from her crossword and a flicker of a smile crosses her face.

I saunter up to her and pull a small, sweet-smelling box out of my jacket pocket. I set it on the counter in front of her.

"Baklava from *moya mama*," I tell her quietly. "With the honey you gifted her."

"Ah, Galina," she says, scooting the box into her lap. "Your mother is a gift herself."

"I agree," I answer, glancing at the security camera. I go on, "Are you okay?"

She nods, her tired green eyes flitting to the door at the back of the room.

"*Da*, not a scratch. Just another night in the office," she says. But I know she's just saying this for the security camera. Zinaida may not be injured, but I'm sure she's a little startled. Not that a stubborn, tough babushka would ever admit it.

"May I use your restroom?" I ask, with another pointed look at the camera.

She gestures to the door. "In the back."

I stride into the back room to find a much less peaceful scene. One young man is being held down by four other men, while the Avtoritet called Gerasim watches over them. The captive is yelling bloody murder, kicking and struggling, but we all know these walls are soundproofed. I recognize him as a recent recruit, a low-ranking Shesty-orka who thought he could trespass the mafia by stealing from Zinaida's register, not realizing she's on the payroll, and not to be fucked with. Especially since she is Arseny's mother, and closest friend to my own mother, Galina.

The men all go quiet when I walk in. Gerasim straightens up and reports, "We've been holding him for you. The Pakhan says you will decide."

"Decide what?" the captive flails.

"Your fate," I answer. "So let me get this straight: not only were you disrespectful of your superiors and your elders, but you were stupid enough to do a sloppy job of it?"

"Caught him worming down the back alley like a coward," says one of the Brodyaga.

"Please! I'm sorry!" the thief wails.

I leer down at him. "I could maybe forgive disrespect or stupidity on their own. But both? In one weak-willed little coward? That I cannot abide. A pity you couldn't make the most of your time in the organization," I say. Then, to Gerasim, "Eliminate him."

"What? No! Please, no!" the young man cries.

"Do it cleanly," I add, turning on my heel to walk away.

I don't look back, even as I hear the crunch of bones breaking and the thief's agonized scream. I step into the main room of the gas station, the door closes, and the only sounds I hear are the soft pop song playing overhead and the scratch of Zinaida's pencil on her crossword. As I'm walking out, she gives me a little wave.

"You're a good boy, Zak," she says in her thick accent. "Be safe."

"I do my best," I tell her as I step out into the crisp October morning.

I climb into my sedan and start the drive back toward

the city. The next several hours are filled with less exciting check-ins with my Avtoritets. Business as always. Throughout the day, my mind returns again and again to Hartley. I can't shirk my duties, but I'm counting down the hours until I go back to the safehouse. In the evening, when the sun is setting, I drive out to a semi-abandoned industrial park in Queens for my last check-in of the day.

I pull up to the predetermined location, just a set of coordinates on a dark dirt road. I flash my lights twice. There's a pause, and then I see the same pattern flash down the way. Just as planned, a caravan of three vehicles pulls into the moonlight. Arseny steps out of the first car, and I do the same. He hands me a briefcase, which I put in the trunk. It's a simple cash drop.

"How is she?" Arseny asks in a low voice.

"Zinaida is perfectly fine. No injuries," I report.

"And the thief?" he prompts.

"Not going to be a problem anymore," I assure him. "I have to commend your ability to carry out orders while concerned for your mother's safety. The Pakhan will be impressed with your loyalty and ambition."

"Thank you," Arseny says softly. "I'm just relieved she's alright."

"Your mother is tough like mine. It'll take more than one cowardly little thief to rattle those old bones," I tell him.

"True," he agrees.

"Back to your post," I tell him.

I turn to leave, ignoring the next question in his eyes. I know he wants to ask about Hartley. But we both know I technically outrank him. If I want to talk about it, I will bring it up. Not the other way around. Besides, I'm impatient to get back to her.

And when I do, I realize it's just in time. I check the security monitors to find that Hartley has her blindfold off, the whole bedroom is tossed, and she's frantically trying to tug the locked door open. I wonder how long she's been at this, maybe all day.

How dare she try to escape my grasp a second time? I grit my teeth, grab a length of rope from a utility closet, and unlock the door to her cell. I hear her gasp and stumble back as I turn the knob. I stand in her doorway, rope in hand, looming over my beautiful, helpless captive.

CHAPTER 8

HARTLEY

It took me a long while to fall asleep after he left me again. I still don't know how much time has actually passed, though. In this room, there is no way to tell time. No alarm clock with bright digital numbers glowing in the dark. No ticking analog on the wall to prove how many hours I have spent in captivity. There isn't even a window to let in the daylight. It could be nighttime. It could be days later. Trapped here in this cell, I have no idea.

All I do is know that it was late afternoon when he captured me. I can vaguely summon up the feeling of wobbling down that dimly-lit alleyway. I remember the way my legs buckled beneath me, the sensation of powerful arms folding around me as I fell. If I force myself back to that moment, I can recall there was still light in the sky. But after that, it's just darkness.

I don't know how long it took me to come to after he drugged me, but I suspect he's kept me here overnight, at least. I think it was morning when he came to me, when he left again. If so, then I spent the entirety of today frantically searching around my cell. I didn't sleep at all last night, so after what must have been hours of tossing the room for any sign of escape, the stress and exhaustion caught up to me. I did finally collapse into a fitful nap on the bed. My body is overwhelmed with the need for rest.

But even then, my troubled mind wouldn't let me rest. I fell right into a dark dream, but more like a memory, with the edges all blurred…

I am standing in a bedroom like this one, only bigger. There are posters of ponies and kittens on the wall, and a pink and purple rug on the floor. The bed is a four-post, just like the one here, only with a pastel pink floral bedspread and a collection of stuffed animals gathered against the pillows. There's no phone, no computer, no clock. There is a window to let in the sun, but instead of coming through bright and shiny, it only illuminates the carpeted floor in narrow shafts of light.

My heart is heavy as I drag my feet forward, closer and closer to that window. I feel so small as I reach for the curtain pull. The pink ruffled curtains draw back, and the bright lines of light fall across my face. I lean in and squint, desperately trying to see out the window through the breaks in the metal bars.

I close one eye, tilt my head, move an inch over. I strain my eyes and my neck trying to see what's going on in the cul-de-sac down below. I can still see it clearly, if only through a narrow gap: the neighborhood kids gathering in the street to play a game. There are four or five kids around my age puttering around on bicycles or roller skates. Girls and boys play harmoniously together. I can still hear their peals of laughter and bits of their excitable conversation as they play their little game. In my dream, sometimes the window opens up and I magically float down to the street to join them.

But most of the time, I still have my face pressed to the metal bars when I wake up, feeling panicked and small.

It's a dream I've had a hundred times before since running away from home, and like all bad dreams, it lingers even after I open my eyes.

The ache of being left out, not by the other kids, but by my own restrictive parents. The loneliness of standing at that barred window, gazing through the cracks at the normal, happy lives going on down below. The pervasive fear that someone is always watching me, always keeping tabs, always noting my mistakes to punish me for later on.

But like I said, it's not just a dream. It's a memory. Those bars on my bedroom window were real.

I was only seven years old when Daddy had the metal bars installed. Only seven when he caught me playing hopscotch at the end of our driveway with the neighbor boy and lost his patience for me. My mother had allowed me outside to play—against the rules—while Daddy was out of town on business, as he often was. But then he came home early. He found me with sidewalk chalk dust on my hands and the boy next door asking my name, asking if we can be best friends. I had never had a friend before. I was going to ask him what it meant.

But then Daddy's Cadillac came rolling up the road. He parked at a sloppy angle, the tires squealing. Before I could run to greet him, he came hurtling out of the SUV. He snatched me up by the arm and carried me into the house, squirming and crying. He called me a whore. He told me I was too young to leave him yet. He hurled accusation after accusation at me—and my mother—which I didn't understand then. I hardly understand it now, why he was so angry. He saw his possession slipping out of his hands. He felt me push back against the rules just a little bit, just innocently, and it was enough to mark me a harlot at age seven.

I tasted one morsel of freedom and normalcy before he closed me back into my frilly pink bedroom and put those bars on the window to keep me in, and keep the world out.

I used to dream about cutting the bars and escaping.

It's no wonder I chose to flee my master's house through the window.

I only wish I could do that now.

When I woke up, I was so disoriented. I thought I was still in my childhood bedroom at home in Wisner, not even my Bronx apartment. I was terrified to be that little girl again, until I realized what was actually going on. I'm here in this holding cell, kept captive by the man who awakened such wild desires in me. And strangely… I'm less afraid to wake up here than I was to wake up in Wisner. At least now I'm a grown-up. At least the man who's holding me hostage now brings me pleasure along with the pain.

Though there is a voice in the back of my head asking the ugly question: Is my family somehow involved in all this? Are they the reason for my captivity yet again? I've been running from my past all this time, but has it finally caught up to me?

That awful thought has hung over me as I search my cell for any signs of weakness. Waking up from that dream was a terrible feeling, but I know I can't wait around for someone to save me. I have to get up and move. I have to try. I feel the walls, listen with my ear pressed against it. I explore the bathroom, stare into the mirror at myself. I search the floor for wobbly floorboards, but it's only tile. Even the dresser is mounted to the wall. There are no decorations. No excess to be found in any form. It's just a simple bedroom and bathroom, cut off from the rest of the universe. It's maddening.

And as the hours stretch on, I feel so lonely.

Until I hear his footsteps thumping softly on the floor. My heart races. I'm not alone anymore! I smell his masculine scent, hear him breathing. The door to my cell creaks open and I fall back, staring wide-eyed as he stands in the doorway, masked in shadow. I'm frozen in place, stunned by a combination of fear and anticipation. When I see him brandish the rope, my body starts to tingle. I feel warm all over. Between my legs, I ache for him.

Why doesn't he scare me more? Am I truly so broken that I *like* this?

I wonder if Stockholm Syndrome is a real thing. Could that be me? Am I so desperate for human connection that I'm bonding with my captor?

"You're back," I murmur. "Where did you go? How long have I been here?"

He doesn't say a word. He walks into the room slowly, and I notice a box under his arm.

"Please, sir… master," I correct myself.

He gives me a look of approval, almost a smile. Then, without a word, he leaves the box on the bed and walks back out of the room. I'm so heartbroken I nearly run after him. Tears burn in my eyes.

Just like that, I'm alone again. I waited for him for hours, but he gives me less than a minute together.

Sadly, I decide to inspect the box. It's neatly wrapped

in silver paper, with a beautiful, fancy-looking card affixed to it. I lift it to my nose, breathing in my master's scent. Then, I open the card and read his message.

"Present yourself and I will come," I read.

I turn over the card to see more words written. This time, it's a description of some pose he wants me to do—when I present myself. My heart pounds faster. He wants me to make myself pretty, to subjugate myself for him.

What's worse is that I *want* to do it. I am eager to follow his instructions. I want to find out what reward he has planned for me if I obey.

Maybe my father was right about me. Maybe there's something really wrong with me, and he was just trying to protect me from dangerous men with sinful minds.

The thought tastes vile in my mouth, and a sneer warps my lips.

Whatever I might be now, I certainly wasn't anything but an innocent child back then.

I gingerly poke my fingernails through the wrapping paper to open the box, desperate for a distraction from my troubled thoughts. My eyes get big when I lift out an expensive-looking black lace bodysuit, complete with a velvet blindfold. Alongside it is a sleek, leather collar, and thicker, padded cuffs for my wrists and ankles. I turn over the delicate fabric in my hands, amazed at how delicate it feels. There's not a loose string or crooked seam to be found. It's immaculate.

And it's just my size.

But that's not all. Underneath that, I find a selection of toiletries of similar high quality. There are a few makeup items—a neutral eyeshadow palette, black mascara, and a rose-pink lipstick. Then I find several fragrant bath products in elegant bottles, and it dawns on me what I'm supposed to do. And if it will get him to come back to me… I'll do anything.

I don't know what I'm trying to prove, or what I'm fighting against.

All I know is that I've been achingly lonely for three months, reliving our night together over and over in my mind. He's like a hurricane. Dangerous, and yet if I stay in the perfect spot, he can protect me from everything else.

I carry the box into the bathroom and strip out of my sweater and jeans. Goosebumps spread across my skin as I lean over to start the bath. I pour rose-scented oil into the hot water and watch the liquids swirl and shimmer. Shiny iridescent bubbles foam up under the pounding water pressure. The tub is large enough for me to sink into without my knees poking up, a luxury I don't have in my Bronx apartment.

I sigh with pleasure as the steaming water rushes over my cool skin. The tension in my muscles starts to ebb away as I soak in the floral-scented bath. I dip my head back and comb my fingers through my hair. I use the bottle of shampoo provided, followed by a deep conditioning. I shave my legs and scrub the sweat and tears from my face. I wallow as long as I can stand it in the hot water, until it's almost lukewarm.

Despite the danger of my situation, I feel luxurious.

It seems impossible that I could enjoy this spa-like experience in the midst of a kidnapping. What kind of criminal is thoughtful enough to provide even more than the essentials for his victim?

After I'm sure I've washed away every dot of grime on my body, I finally emerge from the tub dripping and smooth. I wrap a fluffy white towel around myself, then use a separate one to roughly dry my hair. I use a fancy lotion to moisturize my skin, head to toe. I comb out my hair and carefully apply a light, natural look with the makeup provided. My heart is thumping hard when I put on the lace lingerie. The black fabric feels silky against my skin. I don't have to be an expert to know this is pricey stuff. I would never afford this on my own.

But my master gives me only the best.

I almost laugh at the thought.

He's manipulating you, Hartley, I remind myself.

I gaze at my reflection when I'm done, surprised at what I see. I've never worn lingerie before. I've never even gone into a lingerie store. I was always in survival mode; something as frivolous as feeling sexy never came into the picture. Besides, who would I have dressed up for? One of the many boring, immature guys in my college classes? The old man who lives on the first floor of my apartment building? It's silly to even imagine. I thought I would feel silly wearing the outfit, too, but I was wrong.

Instead, I feel beautiful. I feel empowered. I like the way I look, and I'm even more excited to find out if my master likes it too.

I hope he does.

I check the card to make extra sure I know what I'm meant to do, and then I get to work on 'presenting' myself.

Dressed in my black lace bodysuit, I drop down to my knees before the door. I slide the cuffs onto my wrists and ankles. I fasten the collar around my neck and delicately tie the soft velvet blindfold around my head, careful not to smudge my mascara. It feels strange to blind myself. In this crisis situation, I should want all my senses. But if this is what it takes to get Master's attention…

I take a deep breath and rest my hands on my thighs, palms up, just like he describes on the fancy card. In the silence, I wait patiently for my master to return, not knowing what he will do to me when he does.

Chapter 9

Zakhar

After a long day of running up and down between Long Island and Brighton Beach, I could hardly wait to get back to the safehouse. Back to the beautiful, special gift I left for myself. It's a reward for a hard day's work. I sacrifice a lot to carry the responsibility I bear. Stability. Normalcy. Certain creature comforts I must go without for extended periods of time. Those are things I have to give up in exchange for my service to the brotherhood, and for the loyalty I receive in return. I am a good soldier. I don't complain about my work. I don't shy away from the foul acts I must complete.

If it isn't me in this position, second in rank to the Pakhan, someone else will fill the spot. That man is likely to be less competent and more callous than I am. That means more unnecessary suffering for our enemies and trouble for our comrades. I am a cold executioner, but a fair judge. It's exhausting, back-breaking, soul-questioning work most of the time, but if someone has to do it, I would much rather it be me.

But even a man of my caliber has to unshoulder that burden once in a while. As hard as I work on the job, I play even harder.

This dark path I walk gives shape to dark desires, and now that I have found a potential outlet for my cravings, I'm eager to try her out. Every ounce of stress, restraint, and tension I feel is pent-up, ready to be released.

I am always holding back—keeping myself from that last brutal strike, that step just too far. With a gun in my hand, I have to be cautious. With a beautiful girl bending to my dominance, I can let my restrained energy run wild. A measure of restraint is still needed, of course; I don't want to break my new toy. But I am itching to find out what her limits are. How far can I bend her before she snaps?

I could feel her positively quaking with need when I visited her earlier. The girl may try to hide her true feelings, but I can tell how badly she wants me. It goes beyond want—even she doesn't understand that it's a need now. That she will always be yearning for me to touch her, to show her more of what her own body can do. It's one of my favorite parts: unfolding her like a flower new to blooming. She just needs a little nudge, a little help unfurling those pretty petals for her master.

It's hard to step away from her, even just to teach her a little patience. Leaving her that fancy gift is more than an olive branch—it's a test. I want to see how well my little captive can follow directions. I'm rewarded for my own patience by getting to sit in the security room and monitor her actions on multiple screens. I watch as she opens the gift box, her gorgeous eyes lighting up as her fingertips brush across the expensive lace bodysuit. It's a one-of-a-kind piece I had specially designed. I meet a lot of… interesting people in my line of work. Experts, masters of their craft. One such master, whose shop functions partially as a front for the brotherhood, I called upon to create several pieces of lingerie in Hartley's size. Even before I tracked her down to the Bronx and began planning my capture mission, I knew I would find her again. I knew I would make her mine. And once I did, I would have her wear the high-quality lingerie I ordered for her. Three months of yearning and plotting, and now I have my reward.

Hartley does exactly what I predict of her. She strips out of her old clothes and sinks into that fragrant, warm bath. Through the panel of glass in the mirror, I watch her wash her body. She looks like a water nymph, something ethereal I'm not supposed to see. The sparkling suds slide down her back. She combs through her long blonde hair. My eyes rake over her glossy, voluptuous body as she stands before the mirror, putting on makeup.

Just like I expect, she puts on the lingerie and goes to the door. The adrenaline starts pumping in my veins when I see my lovely little captive drop to her knees. She follows my instructions to the letter, resting her delicate hands on her thick thighs while she waits for me to return. Now that she's ready, it's time for us to begin.

I rise and walk out of the security room. I don't try to muffle my footsteps this time. I want Hartley to know I'm coming. Those few seconds of frenzied anticipation will get her good and riled up. I want her blood flowing and her heart pumping. I stop in front of the door, just thinking about what waits for me on the other side. I draw a deep breath and undo the several locks, then creak the door open. I stand in the doorway, looming over the stunning young woman down on her knees, her head tilted down.

I drink in her gorgeous body, the way the black lace bodysuit clings to every curve. Her hair is almost totally dry now. The ends curl ever so slightly around her shoulders. I look closer and see that she has goosebumps all over. She's trembling just a little, like she can't figure out whether to be excited or fearful. Her pose indicates that she is at rest, on display for me, but that she awaits my next command. The silence is deep. I can feel her nerves.

"Three months I've been waiting for this moment," I finally say, breaking the silence.

Hartley startles slightly at my voice. Her eyes widen. I go on.

"You have not made it an easy time for me," I tell her. "But I don't turn away from a challenge. I am a man who gets what he wants, and I've decided I want you. A million pretty girls in this city, but you, Hartley, are my selection. What a lucky little slut you are."

She swallows hard. I fight back a smile. I reach down to caress her cheek. She sighs and tries to nuzzle into my hand, but as soon as she moves an inch, I pull back. Her brows knit with a pained expression, wondering what she did wrong.

"It is your job to listen. Only I can touch," I explain. I begin to walk in a slow circle around my kneeling captive. "My rules are simple: you do as you're told, and I will reward your obedience with endless pleasure. Defy me, and you will pay the consequences."

I let her sweat out what the consequences could be. I learned a long time ago on the job that you don't have to give it all away. Sometimes, it's more effective to let your subject come up with the answer. Whatever she's imagining is probably worse than anything I could threaten her with. But I will learn her fears soon enough, just the same as I learn her desires. For now, I have just one question for her.

"Are you ready to behave now?" I ask in a low, rough voice.

Hartley nods her pretty head and manages to choke out the words, "Yes, Master."

My cock twitches at the sound of her sweet voice forming those words. I crouch down in front of her, close enough to hear her breathing fast and hard. I reach out and touch her face. This time, she obediently sits still, even when I slide my hand down her neck. I gently wrap my fingers around her throat while I look her up and down. I apply light pressure, just enough to make her heart beat faster. I turn her head from side to side. I caress her bare shoulders and run my fingers through her hair, tugging slightly. I inspect her like a piece of meat or a prized cow, making her feel exposed, on display for me.

"Perfect. Just perfect," I murmur as I trail my fingertips down between her full breasts. All the while, she sits perfectly still in that same pose. I enjoy being hidden from her, watching her without being seen, but my other hand finds the knot on the blindfold and I tug it loose, letting the fabric drift away.

She blinks as her eyes readjust to the light, and I take her chin between my fingers and force her to look me in the eyes.

"You belong to me now," I tell her. "I had this lingerie set made special for you, my sweet little *kukla*. Let's see how you wear it."

I take her hands in mine, lifting them up. Hartley looks utterly fascinated as I bind her ankles and her wrists, the cuffs linking together. I move back and stand up. I snap my fingers and Hartley raises up on her knees with her wrists together in front of her, like she's begging. Like she's praying to me. Behind her, both ankles are bound. She's utterly helpless, dependent on my mercy to survive. I take a few steps back toward the four-post bed. I curl my finger, beckoning for her to come closer.

Hartley balks for a few seconds, looking back at her bound ankles and down at her wrists, then back up at me. Like she can't believe what I'm asking of her. But she doesn't complain. Instead, she carefully braces herself on the floor with her palms, then slowly begins to crawl in my direction.

"Look at me," I remind her sharply. Her eyes flit up to mine, and she doesn't even blink while she inches over to the bed, totally vulnerable before me. I stroke her soft hair.

I bend down to lift her into my arms. She lets out a little yelp of surprise as I scoop her up easily and toss her on the bed. I can see her nipples poking through the thin fabric of her bodysuit. When I slip my hand between her thighs, I feel her warmth. She's getting wet for me already. I cluck my tongue.

"You love the way it feels, don't you?" I growl with approval. "You love being my pretty little slave, Hartley. You know it in your heart, this is what you were born to do. You were created for my pleasure alone."

She nods fervently. "Yes. I-I'm yours," she mutters, her head tilting away in embarrassment. She's not lying to me, she's just confused about how that could be the truth.

I'll teach her, in time.

"That's right," I hiss.

I unhook her ankles and grab them each in my hands. I separate her legs so that they're wide open, and tug her down to the end of the bed. I fasten each ankle to a bedpost and sit on the edge of the bed, between her legs. Hartley's chest rises and falls quickly now as her fear and lust melt together. She's panting hard when I lean in to unclasp her wrists. She looks confused by the sudden freedom.

"That's right. Your hands are free. But you are not allowed to touch yourself… or me," I quickly explain. "If you cannot control your hands, I will bind them again and leave you here."

"Yes, Master," Hartley whispers. Her fingers curl in as she tries her best not to let her hands touch anything at all.

"Such a good girl," I croon. "I think you deserve a little treat."

My hands smooth down her sides. I let my fingertips explore her taut stomach, the swoop of her waist, and the swell of her tits. They're tightly restrained in the bodysuit, with ample cleavage spilling over the top. I grope her breasts and tweak her perky nipples, eliciting a soft moan from her throat. I slip the bodysuit down her shoulders, grabbing her hands as I tug the lingerie down. Her tits pop free, and I lean in to flick my tongue over one nipple while I roll the other between my thumb and forefinger.

My free hand grazes down her body to cup her warm, damp mound. She shivers when my fingers brush over her aching folds, still covered by that thin lacy fabric. I begin to stroke up and down lightly, feeling the way she clenches and pushes against my touch. The poor girl is drenched by now, soaking through the crotch of her bodysuit. I feel the tension in her inner thighs as her legs are held open for me. Her hands instinctively move to touch me, but then she remembers the rule and snatches them back. She struggles to find a place to put her hands as I rub her clit through the fabric. Hartley's plush lips fall open. She's sighing and twitching in my grasp, writhing with need. I massage the sensitive hood of her clit while she arches into my hand, whimpering incoherent noises. Her eyes start to roll back with pleasure, but I bring her back with a sharp, quick smack on the cheek.

"Don't close your eyes. Look at me," I command her.

Hartley is obedient, managing to hold eye contact even as I torture her with delicate touches. She's squirming underneath me now, and I can tell she's on the verge of coming. But before she can reach the climax, I move my hand away. She twinges, gasping for air. Just as the tension is ebbing away, I slip my hand between her thighs again. I brush up and down, circling her clit with each pass. Hartley's hands tighten into fists and she reaches out to clasp the bedsheets. I tease her like this again and again, bringing her close to the edge, only to pull back.

The poor girl is desperate for a release. Her cheeks are flushed, her eyes watering, her mouth salivating. Her whole body trembles as I finger her and grope her tits. I lean forward and kiss her on the cheek, whispering in her ear.

"So close, aren't you? Almost there, my little pet."

"Please," she gasps. "I-I need it."

"You need to come. I know. Your pussy is begging to burst all over my fingers. Is that what you want, Hartley? Are you ready for me to make you come?" I growl.

She nods breathlessly.

"I'm going to show you just how good it is to be mine," I tell her between gritted teeth.

Instead of simply slipping the bodysuit to one side, I reach down with both hands and tear the fabric at her crotch, ripping it open. I don't care at all that the bodysuit costs more than most people pay for rent. It's just window dressing for the real gift, the true beauty underneath. As I breathe in her delicious feminine fragrance, my cock twinges. I gaze down at Hartley's bare pussy glistening with honey and reach to unzip my pants, preparing to take my prize.

CHAPTER 10

HARTLEY

My chest aches with every resounding thump of my heart. Every single cell in my body seems to be ringing with stimulation. I twitch and squirm under my master's expert touch, losing my mind in the soup of adrenaline and pleasure chemicals. It's almost too much for me to handle, like I'm simply receiving too much at once. Compared to the long hours alone in this empty room, staring at the walls in silence, this is a smorgasbord of emotions and sensations.

I feel the beads of sweat forming along my spine and the slick juices dripping down my sticky thighs. My abdominal muscles tense with every move I make, and my arms feel heavy from constantly holding back the urge to use my hands. The collar feels tighter around my neck as I strain, and I'm aware of the ache in my ankles, not from the soft cuffs themselves, but from the tension of holding my legs wide open. I've always been a pretty flexible person, made even more so by years of yoga warm-ups before cardio sessions, but holding this position for a prolonged amount of time is slightly painful even for me.

Of course, the ache in my muscles would probably be less intense if I wasn't perpetually straining closer to him. I can't help but gravitate to him, leaning into his every touch, whether it's a gentle one or not. In the back of my mind, an alarm bell rings. It's a reminder that I'm not in control here, that I'm at the mercy of this mysterious man who could break me in half without breaking a sweat.

I hate how he makes me feel, but I have no choice but to surrender.

It's what I want to do.

Maybe I really am broken, trusting in this monster to fix me.

But Master seems to know intuitively what my body can and cannot handle, and he knows how to push me to the brink without falling over the edge.

I hardly want to take the time to blink and risk missing a second of his impressive body moving over me. I drink in his heavily-muscled chest and back, his arms and legs thick enough to crush me between them. His skin is smooth and glossy with a faint sheen of sweat, which only defines his musculature and adds to his intoxicating masculine scent.

I can see here and there the faintest remnants of old scars. In between the waves of mind-melting pleasure and pain, I wonder how he got those scars. How many ancient wounds has he had to heal from? What kind of life does he lead to fall into such suffering again and again? I can only speculate about the battles he's won… and how bad the other guys must have looked by comparison.

The scars remind me again to be careful. Even in the

depths of immense ecstasy, I have to keep my hands to myself like my master instructed. If the reward for being good feels like *this*, then I can only assume the punishment must be as hellish as the reward is heavenly. Besides, I don't want to disobey—I want to be a good girl. I want to be everything he asks of me. I will be the perfect captive, the ideal submissive. Anything to keep him touching me.

He looks down at me with fire blazing in his dark eyes. I hold my breath in anticipation. The cool air wafts over my bare slit and I whimper, lifting my hips to meet him. Begging him without a word to please, please fuck me. He admires my pussy, pushing the ripped fabric of the bodysuit to each side. Careful not to make any mistakes with my hands, I brace myself to look down at the space between us. My heart beats faster when I hear him unzip his pants. I lick my lips and feel the twinge inside me, my hole pleading to be filled. He takes out his stiff, massive cock and begins to slowly stroke it in his hand. He guides the thick, swollen head of his shaft to my pulsing flower and teases the tight band of nerves there. He rubs himself against me and I shiver from head to toe. It feels like the tension inside me is a tightly-wound rubber band, ready to snap at the slightest provocation. Pleasure builds up inside me and threatens to spill over.

The miasma of fear and doubt swirls around me, but the promise of release begins to soothe them away.

"Please," I murmur. "I-I'm almost there."

"You'll come when I say so," he rumbles.

I whimper in protest, but when he lines up and shoves the full aching length of his cock inside of me in one smooth, forceful push, I gasp. Mingled pain and delight shoot up through my core. I'm overwhelmed with the sensation of fullness, of being utterly stuffed with my master's cock.

He's so big, he can only barely sheathe himself completely with my pussy. He presses in as deeply as he can. The head of his cock pokes into a spot inside of me that feels like heaven. His heavy balls slap against my ass, and I feel him pulsating inside me. Every twinge makes my pussy ache for release.

At this point, I'm desperate to come, and yet it's like my body won't even allow it. Not until Master says it's time.

"This pussy is mine. All mine," he growls, and I whine in acknowledgment. It listens to him better than it listens to me.

"I want you to come for me now, Hartley."

He rocks his hips just a little, creating delicious friction without pulling out even an inch. The engorged head of his cock brushes into that sweet spot again, and I nearly forget how to breathe. I cry out as all the world goes black for a moment. Fireworks explode behind my eyes. My pussy clenches tightly around his shaft, pumping him with every twitch of ebbing ecstasy. His hands grasp my hips. I feel his fingernails dig into my soft flesh as he slides his length almost completely out of me, then slams back into my cervix again. Master pumps in and out of my pussy hard and fast, pounding my g-spot again and again.

Another orgasm builds inside me, and just as I'm tensing for release, he withdraws from me. But instead of going away, that little seed of pleasure grows bigger and bigger as he smacks my pussy with the palm of his hand. I writhe and twitch with pleasure, edged with the most sumptuous lick of pain. For what feels like forever, he alternates between plunging his cock deep inside of me and pulling out to slap my pussy.

I bite my lip, my eyes watering as I hurtle toward another climax. It takes all my brainpower to remember to keep my hands to myself. Logic and reason are starting to disappear. Nothing makes sense to me anymore except for this—his cock inside of me, his body controlling mine. He smacks my pussy while I moan and melt into his hand. I come again, drenching his fingers and cock with my slick juices.

"Ohh my god," I breathe raggedly.

"That's right, come all over my cock," he commands.

He pumps into me hard and fast, pummeling my g-spot while his pelvis creates friction against my clit. Our bodies slide together in perfect harmony, with my master in control of the whole scene. My legs are still spread-eagled apart and trembling from the force of multiple orgasms. I lose count after the fourth, as the bliss melds together into one continuous wave. My hands twist in the bedsheets. My toes curl at the bedposts. My handsome captor gazes down into my eyes with an intensity that makes me blush, even with his cock buried inside me. There's not an ounce of shame or regret in his gaze. He doesn't feel bad for keeping me captive. He doesn't feel guilty for using my body like an expensive, pretty sex toy. And instead of frightening me, his confidence makes me feel strong, too. Like I must be something pretty damn special to deserve this reward. Surrendering to him feels like a win for me somehow. He knows how to make my body feel good—even better than I do.

I get swept away in those dark brown eyes and momentarily forget the rule he set earlier. Acting on pure instinct, I reach up to touch his hard chest with my trembling hands. It's halfway between a caress and a push, like I can't decide whether I want to melt into him or escape his grasp. Either way, I have broken the rules, and he responds instantly.

"What did I tell you?" he growls sharply.

In one large hand, he grabs my wrists together and pins them up over my head. Now, not only are my legs immobilized by the ankle cuffs, but I have to surrender control of my arms. I'm completely held down, utterly in his control. I'm afraid of what he'll do to me for a second, bracing for some kind of pain. But the only pain he gives me is the fulfilling ache of his cock slamming into my cervix. It's been a long, long time since he last fucked me like this, and my body is out of practice. The prolonged force and friction is starting to sting, but in the best way possible. I can already imagine how long I'll be aching for after he's done with me. I almost look forward to admiring the bumps and bruises left behind, physical proof that my master fucked my brains out. When he inevitably leaves me again, at least I'll have these visceral memories to dwell in while I wait.

His hand tightens around my wrist, the other hand bracing himself as he pounds my pussy with his glorious cock. I'm so wet, he slides in and out with ease. I can feel him tensing up, his teeth gritting together. He's almost to the edge now, too, and I find myself desperate for it. I want him to fill me up more than anything. I stare back into his eyes, meeting his intensity with my own. I clench my pussy around his thickness and he groans, quickening the pace. His cock spears into me with abandon, his hips snapping back and forth.

"Don't you ever forget who you belong to," he hisses.

"I'm yours, Master. All yours," I gasp.

Master pummels my cunt hard and fast a few moments more, and then I feel his whole body seize up. His cock pumps hot, precious seed inside of me, and I squeeze out every drop. It makes me come again, just feeling him pulse inside me. My juices mingle with his, dribbling from my slick, aching pussy. He holds himself there for a long moment, like he's making sure to empty himself completely. Finally, he pulls out and leans down, kissing my cheek as he noses through my hair.

"My perfect little whore," he murmurs in my ear.

In between the pangs of pleasure, my mind hurtles back in time to another, totally separate moment. I see my father's face contorted with anger, his lips spitting the word 'whore' as he looms over my tiny frame. The memory stings like a wasp most of the time, but tonight it just floats into my mind and flutters back away. The word feels less like an insult and more like a term of endearment. It strikes me how bizarre it is that the man I called 'daddy' treated me like a commodity to be hoarded, and the man I call 'master' treats me like something precious. My father never spoiled me with pretty things. He only made me cry alone in my room. At least Master makes my eyes water with pleasure, not pain.

He strokes my face, bringing me back to the present moment. Now that it's over, I realize just how exhausted I am. I can only lie on the bed, limp, as he uncuffs my ankles. He massages them gently and pushes my aching legs back together. He slips the torn bodysuit down my legs and drops it to the floor. I'm helpless as he scoops me into his strong arms and carries me to the bathroom. He rests me on the edge of the tub while he fills it with steamy water and more of that rose-scented oil. I can't manage a single word; I'm so overwhelmed with exhaustion and emotion. But I don't need to speak. Master and I don't need words.

He slides me into the hot bath and gets to work washing my tired body. He gently lathers the soap on my sweaty skin, even working the shampoo into my hair. I can only sit in stunned silence as the man I once feared enough to flee down a fire escape now cares for me with all the tenderness of a real lover. It hits me that I've never been touched like this before—not for as long as I can remember. Master isn't ashamed, and neither am I. If anything, I feel a pinch of shame for… *not* feeling ashamed of our rough, forceful love-making. But it dawns on me that this is just old baggage, old wounds I carry around from my childhood. My father always made it clear that having sex reduced my value. Giving it up for a man meant betraying my father. My body is a gift to be given, and I am supposed to mean nothing once I give it.

However, my master doesn't make me feel worthless. In fact, even in my limp state, I feel more empowered than before. If this aggressive, forceful man is willing to regard me with softness after everything we did together, it must mean I'm still valuable somehow. Even more enlightening, I realize that he doesn't *have* to do this. No one would stop him if he simply fucked me and left me there alone, sticky with his come and cuffed to the bed. He's choosing to take care of me. I wish it would go on forever.

But once I'm thoroughly cleansed, he gently dries me off and carries me back to the bed. At first, I think there's a chance he's going to stay with me, until I see the way he's tucking me in. My heart sinks, knowing I'm about to be alone again. I don't want to be locked in a bedroom alone with my thoughts. It reminds me of being a little kid, peering through those bars on my window, wishing someone would come save me.

And it's a reminder that my master is not my boyfriend, he's my captor. He may care for me, but he's the one who gets to come and go. No matter how I feel about him, I have to be realistic about the outcome here. He has obviously captured me for a reason, and I would be naive to think it has only to do with sex.

As he's walking back to the door, preparing to leave me behind, I sit up in bed. He looks back at me. Waiting for me to say something. My heart is pounding, but I manage to speak up.

"You know, if you're holding me here because you think my family will pay to get me back, you're mistaken," I tell him bravely. "Because I was dead to them the second I left home."

Chapter 11

Zakhar

There's a crispness to the air as I stroll down the boardwalk. It's late October, just a few days before Halloween. I pull up the collar of my black leather jacket as a sharp breeze rolls over me. It brings with it the salty brine of the sea mingled with the scents of hot dogs, nachos, and sunscreen. It's noon on a Wednesday, definitely not peak hour for Coney Island attractions, but there are still throngs of tourists and locals alike. They come all the way here for a taste of the good old days, or just a break from the tightly-packed urban environment. Every sign, every mural, every design out here reminds me of a bygone era, a time people tend to call 'simple'. I have enough life experience to understand that nothing is simple. Even this place, drenched in nostalgia, is just another potential setting for a very modern crime.

I look out over the beige sandy beach, at the scattered groups of sun-worshippers soaking up the last tolerable days of early winter before the coastal winds get too harsh.

I see them huddled in little masses with their blankets and snacks. Teenagers cutting class for a midweek gossip sesh. Families from out of town with their fanny packs and diaper bags. Just past them, the dark gray water laps at the shore. A tiny child wobbles toward the water's edge and a young mom with a flouncy blonde ponytail goes hurrying after to scoop him up. Watching them together gives me a strange ache in my heart. It feels like yearning, but I'm not sure what for.

My mind inevitably clicks back to Hartley. Now, *that's* yearning if I've ever felt it. Being apart from her feels unnatural. Like I'm betraying some law of nature by leaving her behind. Especially with her words from last night still lingering in my mind.

"I was dead to them the second I left home."

After she told me that, I made sure not to react outwardly. I need her to understand who's in control. I can't have her thinking she can ruffle my feathers. I try to keep my emotions as blank as possible. It's safer that way. The less she knows, the better. At least for now, while I'm still working on her. She's not ready for the full truth yet.

But her statement makes me wonder what she's running from. What could be so bad that she would rather live in the shadows, under a false name, denying herself pleasure and true freedom, than return home?

I stop in front of a towering green gate with a creepy-looking man's face looming over it. The words SCREAM ZONE are emblazoned in red light bulbs around his head. The expression on his pale face evokes a predatory hunger rather than a promise of a good, wholesome time. The gates are open, with a steady trickle of customers coming through wearing sunglasses, visors, and backpacks. It's the entrance to Luna Park, an old-fashioned amusement park renamed for the original that used to stand there nearly a hundred years ago.

I step aside and lean against the orange pillar, looking as inconspicuous as possible while scanning the crowds for my partner on today's mission. I glance at my wristwatch just as the long hand ticks noon. The sun is directly overhead, but hidden behind a knot of storm clouds. The atmosphere is changing with the weather. People on the beach are packing up to leave. Those loitering along the boardwalk find streetside restaurants or shops to step into before the rain comes. It's better this way. The fewer tourists hanging around, the fewer potential witnesses there will be to deal with.

My partner for the day, Gerasim, comes strolling up to me. He looks like the epitome of 'low-key' in his all-gray tracksuit and black hoodie. He wears a black cap with the bill tugged down low over his forehead. He gives me a curt nod and stands to the side with me while a couple of middle-aged tourists waddle through the park entrance.

"Right on time," I greet him in a low voice.

"Wouldn't leave you hanging," he replies. "Thanks again for your help yesterday."

"I assume your guys cleaned up after themselves?" I mutter.

He nods, a fleeting smile crossing his face. "As if Zinaida would let us leave a mess in her back room," he jokes darkly. "Don't worry. You'd never know what happened there."

"Excellent. The Pakhan will be impressed with your

work ethic and attention to detail," I say, as I gesture for him to follow me into Luna Park.

Gerasim straightens up his posture, like the mere mention of the Pakhan is enough to put him on edge. We walk through the green gates, keeping our footsteps soft. The storm clouds rumble overhead, promising a downpour. I don't mind. A little rain would clear out the remaining tourists and give us some cover.

"Speaking of the Pakhan," he begins softly, "can you give me any insight on today's mission? What does he think of my hunch?"

"I don't think he's surprised to hear that Yury is causing trouble again. Disappointed, I'm sure, but he has no reason to doubt your information," I assure him. "That is, unless you're having second thoughts?"

Gerasim shakes his head. "No, no. To tell you the truth, I've had my eye on this kid for a while. I know I'm the newest Avtoritet, and I don't want to speak out of turn, but I *know* I'm doing a better job than Yury. It's not just that he's young, either. Twenty is old enough to fall into line, but he's sloppy. He's inconsistent. His own *Brodyaga* report that he is impossible to reach much of the time. Not to be a snitch, but I question his loyalty to the organization."

"Your instincts have proven accurate so far. And we all know the circumstances of Yury's recruitment are… dubious," I put it lightly.

Gerasim tightens his fists and scoffs. I understand his righteous rage.

Nepotism of any kind is rare in the organization. We do all we can to sniff it out and eliminate it. There's no place for that kind of unearned favoritism. But Yury's grandfather is a pillar of the Brighton Beach community and an old friend of the Pakhan, despite not being a part of the Bratva himself. Yury has been a troublemaker known to police in the neighborhood for years. Petty theft, assault, and finally possession got him arrested two years ago when he was freshly turned eighteen. The cops on our payroll collaborated with Yury's influential grandfather and the Pakhan to create an alternative to the prison sentence awaiting him. He would dedicate his life to the brotherhood in exchange for a second chance. Running his own team of *Boyeviks* was meant to teach him responsibility, loyalty, and the value of hard work.

"A miraculous gift the Pakhan granted him, and all Yury has done is squander it," my partner grumbles. "Even his own men don't trust him."

"The kid is accused of taking money from the Obshchak fund. His 'business' dealings have brought in considerably less money than in past years," I recount.

"I just know he's using that money for drugs. Buying, selling, whatever it is—that's not his money to spend. God knows he didn't earn a cent of it himself," Gerasim quips. "Yury hasn't gotten his hands dirty in two years of service."

"We'll know soon enough whether he's back to his old ways," I agree.

I don't have to mention the second part of the statement: that if we do find him in the midst of a drug deal, as suspected, his notable parentage won't help him.

"I'm glad to have you here. The Pakhan trusts you. I would never be able to pull this off without you vouching for me," Gerasim says.

Before I can respond, my senses suddenly sharpen. The

hairs on the back of my neck stand up. I put my arm out in front of Gerasim to stop him. I hold my breath, focusing all my attention on my surroundings. We stand perfectly still, our eyes scanning the park. Up ahead is a carousel, churning out an eerily upbeat tune while the gilded horses bob up and down in an endless circle. Fat raindrops patter the ground. The park is nearly deserted by now, with just a few stragglers trying to ride out the rain.

But I ignore them, because on the other side of the carousel is Yury, standing there in a hoodie and oversized jeans. He rolls back and forth on his heels as he peers around. His highly reflective aviator sunglasses do little to hide his demeanor. In fact, they make him stand out more, because who wears polarized sunglasses on a rainy day? Even with his eyes covered, I can tell how nervous he is. I see the tension in his jaw. He anxiously runs his fingers through his grown-out brown hair. He licks his lips and swallows multiple times, like his mouth is dry.

A lanky, sketchy-looking man in a long coat comes shuffling up to Yury. They exchange a few hushed words, then the man passes Yury what looks like a thick packet of paperwork. The young Avtoritet hands him a thick wad of cash.

"That little prick," Gerasim growls from over my shoulder. "I knew it."

Once the lanky man slinks away, we watch Yury tuck the packet into his hoodie. As he turns to walk away, Gerasim and I exchange a wordless understanding. Careful to keep to the shadows, we move around the carousel and begin following the kid through the amusement park. We stay back until we're far enough away from the other patrons to make a move.

"Yury," I say in a firm voice. "Stop. It's over."

I can see the panic on his face even with his shades on. He murmurs, "Oh shit."

Then, he bolts.

"Motherfucker!" Gerasim hisses.

We break into a run, chasing Yury through the maze of carnival games and rusty old rides. The kid is running for his life, but that's not good enough. We corner him in front of the Spook-a-Rama, with fake skeletons looming behind him in the window. Yury skids to a stop and whirls around, looking petrified as Gerasim and I close in on him. With a trembling hand, the kid whips a knife out of his hoodie and brandishes it.

"Don't come any closer!" he cries out.

But Gerasim is an unstoppable force. He barrels straight for Yury and tackles the kid to the filthy ground. With Gerasim on top of him, Yury makes a wild stab toward the man's face, which slices across his cheek. Gerasim bellows with pain and rage as a bright red spurt of blood splatters the pavement. His hand reflexively snaps away to touch his bloody face, giving Yury just enough time to make another trembling jab. This time, the blade pierces Gerasim's shoulder. He jerks his injured arm back, but uses his other shoulder to pound down into Yury's chest. The young man gasps as the air is knocked from his lungs, his eyes bulging out of his head. The knife goes clattering away and I run to snatch it up before racing to Gerasim and Yury, who are grappling for control. The older Avtoritet is pissed off, pummeling the young kid in the gut while Yury groans in the fetal position.

"Stop! Police!" shouts a deep voice from a short distance behind us.

"They're here," I relay to Gerasim, who's now got Yury pinned.

"Fucking finally," Gerasim grunts, and throws another punch to the kid's ribs.

Yury is rolling on the ground in pain, but it's almost over now. The cops on mafia payroll will show up and arrest Yury. He shattered the deal his grandfather made for his life when he used Obshchak funds to buy drugs.

But as the police team comes running around the corner into view, my blood runs cold. I don't recognize a single one of them. These are not the Brighton Beach police we usually deal with. These are Coney Island officers, approaching what looks like a brutal assault by two big, built men on one scrappy twenty-year-old. I quickly determine this is not going to go our way.

I glance over at Gerasim and see that he's put it together too. He grits his teeth and keeps clenched onto Yury's collar, refusing to let the bruised-up kid escape even now.

I look down at the knife, at my palms stained red. There are drops of Gerasim's blood on my shirt. I look just as culpable, maybe more so. But I can't be arrested. It's not a selfish decision; Gerasim and I both know that I hold a more esteemed position in the organization. If I get taken down, the whole brotherhood suffers. I know too much. I'm too close to the Pakhan.

And on a more personal note, if I go down, who will take care of Hartley, who's still locked up alone in the safehouse?

"Go!" Gerasim barks at me. "Run before they reach us!"

I tuck the knife into my jacket and pull it tight around me, hiding the stains on my shirt. The least I can do is take the evidence with me.

"I will fix this," I promise him fiercely as I turn to leave. "I will make this right."

CHAPTER 12

HARTLEY

I lie on the bed in silence, staring up at the ceiling. I have no real basis for what time of day it is… or even what day it is. There is no window to show me the sun or the moon or at the very least, enough natural light to indicate I'm still on planet Earth. Being stuck in a two-room space for a long time is disorienting. The world shrinks down inside my mind. It becomes harder and harder to picture my apartment, or the view out of my tiny kitchen window. I even start to question my own memories. Was that apartment real? Was I really a culinary student in the Bronx, pretending to be a girl named Maggie? Or have I been here all along, trapped in this room which feels like a torture chamber when I'm alone, and a secret, sexy oasis when my master is here with me? Two days or forever, I can't tell how long it's been. Does it even matter?

I wonder if even my newest memories are reliable. My life seems so out of the ordinary. This kind of thing doesn't just happen to people, right? What makes me so special? Why would Master pick someone like me, when I know the city is filled with beautiful women who would be more than willing to submit to him? What about me interests him so much?

I roll over in bed with a sigh, my fingers going up to the leather collar around my neck. I trace the edges as I stare off in thought.

I'm aching to be with him again. I feel so empty when he's not around. Having him inside of me, pumping hard and deep… it's the closest to true satisfaction I have ever known. Not to mention the way he takes care of me afterward. Nobody has ever cared this much about my pleasure, my limits, my well-being.

And this all from a man who drugged my coffee and kidnapped me.

I used to fear his return. Now I wait for it impatiently.

There's a part of me that feels such a depth of shame as I grapple with these strange feelings. I escaped the prison of my parent's making only to find myself excited to be Zakhar's captive. What the hell does that say about me?

I'd definitely lose any feminist cred I had if I admitted my desires aloud.

After all, he picks and chooses when to visit me. And for how long. I'm not in control here, and I should be terrified, yet I've never felt so alive!

I must have fallen asleep sometime after he left me, in what I assume was the nighttime. I woke up 'this morning' to find no Master, but another gift box sitting for me at the door. He must have opened it just a crack to slide in the box while I was sleeping, before leaving again. I'm still kicking myself for missing his visit. I wish I had been awake to see him, even if just for a split second. Instead, I could only pore over the contents of the gift box, sniffing them, holding them close, as though I could extract a little piece of Master's presence somehow.

This time, he brought me food—a hunk of warm, dark bread with a slightly sweet rye fragrance, two shiny apples, a bottle of orange juice, and a small bag of fancy-looking salted nuts. The food items are neatly arranged in a small wicker basket on top of the other items. There's a fancy pair of ivory lace panties, warm knee socks, and an oversized black tee shirt that smells ever so faintly like my master. Of course, I immediately put on the clothing items and devoured the food, since I had been God knows how long without any calories. Not to mention how many I must have burned having rough sex. But since then, I have just been listlessly lying on the bed, letting my mind unravel in the silence.

So when I hear the soft thump of footsteps again, my heart starts pounding. I launch out of bed and rush to the door to listen. Sure enough, I hear him coming closer. I step back from the door, trying to clamp down on my excitement. I hear the click of the multiple locks sliding open, and then the doorknob turns. My whole body is vibrating with anticipation.

The door creaks open and my jaw drops. I stumble back at the sight of my master in the doorway, his shirt splattered with something red… and wet. It takes a full two seconds for my mind to acknowledge that it's blood. I can't see any obvious wounds, so I have to make the frightening assumption that it isn't his own.

On the one hand, I'm relieved he doesn't seem to be hurt.

On the other hand… I'm terrified.

And yet when he comes walking into the room, I freeze

up. I can only stare at him in awe as he approaches me. I feel like a tiny, silly kid in my big tee shirt and panties. I am woefully underdressed and underprepared in comparison to Master, who looks fresh from a battle. There's a light sheen of sweat across his forehead, dampening the hair at his temples.

"Are you afraid?" he rumbles, standing over me.

I gulp. "N-No," I lie.

He opens his leather jacket and draws out a long, glistening knife. My heart skips. My eyes go wide. My mouth falls open as my breathing quickens. He wipes the blade on a clean corner of his shirt. He raises the blade between us, and I see a distorted reflection of my surprised face looking back at me. He leans down to whisper in my ear.

"What about now?"

I can scarcely breathe, much less speak. I nod my head and he gives me a dark smile.

"Say it," he commands.

"I am afraid," I admit, my voice barely audible.

"Good. You should be," he growls.

With the blade still in front of my face, he slides his free hand around to cup the back of my head. He strokes my hair a few times before gathering it into his fist. He gently tugs my hair to tilt my head up, my chin jutting out and my neck exposed. He presses the cold blade flat against my throat, digging just beneath the leather collar. I don't dare even breathe.

"I could destroy you in a heartbeat," he murmurs roughly.

He slowly turns the blade of the knife so that the sharp edge barely scrapes my skin. His other hand slides down my back. He grabs my ass lewdly.

"But why would I ruin something so perfect?" he whispers.

The fear I feel is palpable. Sweat beads on the back of my neck and palms of my hands. My heart thumps hard and fast. The adrenaline pumps through my veins. For a split second, I flash back to the last time I felt such terror.

I was a little girl, scared of her own father. He struck such fear into my heart. He taught me the meaning of pain.

It was why I escaped, the first chance I could.

Even though the feelings he brings up in me are so familiar, they're nothing alike. Master is different. He converts my fright and ache into pleasure. It's a delicious kind of fear, edged with temptation and the promise of gratification. All I have to do is obey, and I will receive the wildest bliss.

It's warped, I know. The scars of my trauma still linger on my psyche, but giving into these desires with him feels… healing. I don't know how or why I can be so certain of something in all of this, but Master will never hurt me. He'll never push me too far.

Which is a pretty fucking extreme gamble, considering I have a blade to my throat. All it would take is just a little bit of pressure, and I'm a goner. And yet, even as adrenaline flushes through me, and my heart races, my pussy throbs with excitement.

He brings up the fear just like my father, but instead of exploiting it, he rewards it, and soothes my aches away.

His eyes bore into mine, dark and hypnotic. He gives a slight jerk of his head, urging me to walk backward as he presses the knife to my neck. I slowly shuffle back, with Master leading me by the knife until I'm pressed against the wall. I'm almost hyperventilating now as I struggle to keep my breaths shallow enough not to disturb the blade.

He turns the knife until the very point is poking into my flesh, then he lightly drags it downward. His other hand reaches to grab my shirt collar. I gasp as he tugs it up, then plunges the knife through the simple cotton fabric. It punctures and he drags it down, slicing the tee shirt down the center of my body. He pulls it through like butter, the fabric stripped into one useless, continuous scrap. He drops it to the ground. I stand exposed, with my bare chest heaving. But he isn't finished yet. I whimper as his fingers hook under the waistband of my panties at my left hip. He runs the knife down my front in a slow, tortuous wave. He slips the knife under the thin lace at my hip, then tears it right through. I'm still frozen stiff as he does the same on the right. The shredded panties fall to the floor, too.

He groans with approval, looking me up and down. Chills spread across my naked skin. My nipples stiffen in the cool air. My pussy tingles between my thighs.

"So beautiful," he purrs. "You're made for me."

With his hand wrapped around the hilt, he presses the knife tip into my soft breast, right over my heart. His other hand caresses its way down to my mound. I suck in a tight breath when his rough, calloused fingertips brush over my clit. He begins to slowly massage the sensitive bundle of nerves in a rhythmic circle. The friction is hard enough to make my heart race, but light enough to tantalize me. He knows exactly what he's doing. The tension builds up inside me bit by bit, edged with the fear of what might happen if that blade slips even an inch.

"The danger makes you hot, doesn't it?" he growls.

I'm so ashamed of how transparent I am to him, and my head bobs as hot, intense tears spring to my eyes. They're not tears of terror, though. He's doing more for me in this moment than months of therapy could ever accomplish.

When he slips two long fingers inside of me, my knees buckle. My body goes weak as he slides in and out of my slick pussy. His dark eyes are locked with mine, the knife still poking into my breast while he fingers me. Pleasure mounts ever higher, especially when he pushes deeper and knocks against my g-spot. Sparkles burst in my eyes and my mouth falls open in a silent 'oh'. Master leans in close and presses his lips to mine. His teeth graze my bottom lip, mirroring the blade as he turns it sideways and presses harder against my skin. His fingers push into me harder and faster, with a sweep up over my thrumming clit every pass.

My racing thoughts are so distant now, as I'm pulled into my body. There is nothing outside of this moment, no past or future. There is no one in the world but us. Buddhist monks spend decades trying to achieve what he's able to with his fingers and a knife, as he takes me to Nirvana.

I'm gasping against his lips, moaning into his mouth as that bead of incredible pleasure grows and grows inside me. I feel a tight, burning sensation, like I'm about to burst, and a prism kaleidoscope dances on the back of my eyelids.

"That's right. Don't hold back, *malyshka*. Let it come," he commands.

And just like that, I do. My body nearly collapses to the floor as the most powerful, gushing orgasm rocks through me. My knees knock together as my pussy clenches around my master's fingers, and a cascade of my own juices comes rushing down my thighs. The knife lays gentle against my chest while he caresses my slick flower through the shockwaves of bliss. I'm lost in the sensations of pleasure, pain, fear, and longing. The endorphins pulse through my veins, making me feel more alive than ever before. All my senses are on fire. All my attention is locked on the man of my filthiest dreams.

I'm still awash in post-climax glow when he growls huskily in my ear, "I've given you a reason to trust me. Now, I need to know if I can trust you."

Chapter 13

Zakhar

My black sedan rolls down a dusty, two-lane county road with the windows a couple inches rolled down to let in the brisk autumn air. I squint into the late afternoon glare. The horizon is turning orange like a glowing ember as the sun dips into the west. My hands slide over the smooth, cool leather of the steering wheel. On either side of the highway, the tree line grows close and dense. The once-green branches are turning to jewel tones of red, gold, and bronze with the season. I am on my way from Manhattan, where I have been running operations all morning, to the Forest Hills area of Long Island. It's not an extremely long distance, but the traffic in NYC is always clogged, especially on a beautiful Friday afternoon just before Halloween. So many city-dwellers are on their way out for the weekend, heading north to the mountains or east to the coast. It takes me a long time to shake loose of the traffic outside of Brooklyn and hit clean air, finally taking my foot off the brake to hit the gas.

It's a peaceful break from the pollution-choked streets

of New York City, like slipping through the veil into another world. I welcome the opportunity for a little fresh air and space, even though I'm completely in my element in the city, too. I can handle anything, any place, but if I have a choice… I like the scenery out here a little better. And the privacy—or at least the illusion of it—is almost enough to let me relax. I have passed maybe three or four other vehicles during the latter part of the multi-hour drive from the city. I can almost pretend I'm alone out here, free to wander wherever I please.

But I would be a fool to believe that. There is no real safe place. There is no peace. Not in the world I inhabit. Not in my line of work. The Pakhan has eyes everywhere, and I have to assume our enemies do, too. An attack could come from any direction at any time. If I don't watch my back, someone is likely to stab it. And they may even be one of my many brothers.

In fact, that is the reason for my drive out to Forest Hills today. The Pakhan wants to meet with me to discuss what went down at Coney Island a day and a half ago. I know the man fairly well at this point, so I'm not filled with as much dread as one might expect, on my way to meet with the ultimate authority of the organization. He regards me with enough respect to request a meeting one-on-one instead of sending a middleman to 'discuss' with me. Or even worse, simply ordering my head on a platter. A lower-ranked Boyevik would just probably meet the hollow end of a gun and nobody would bat an eye.

I'm lucky to be in my position, but I've earned it, too. I remind myself of that fact as I pull off onto an exit ramp in the middle of nowhere. The car purrs as I tap the brakes, and I look around to find a deserted-looking old fuel station and a tiny, weathered diner, with nothing else surrounding but trees for miles. I turn into the lot and back into a space beside a curb. There are a few other cars at the diner, including a shadowy, dark silver BMW double-parked at the side of the small building. There's a man sitting in that car, barely visible behind the dark tinted windows, just waiting in the driver's seat. The Pakhan's personal chauffeur. He glances over at me and gives the faintest nod.

That's my cue.

I turn off the engine, take a deep breath, and step out of the car. The cold wind folds around me and I zip up my leather jacket. I walk toward the entrance of the diner, already hearing the muffled strains of a country-blues warbler on the jukebox. Bells above the door jingle when I walk in.

Inside, the place looks like a fading movie set from the fifties. The diner has a long, chrome-colored counter and several red pleather booths. The floors are a mottled hard-wood, and the fluorescent light panels overhead cast the restaurant in a pale glow. There's one middle-aged wait-ress with steel-gray hair in a no-nonsense bun and old-timey apron. She does a double take when I walk in. I see her eyes roll up and down my body, and her eyebrow lifts with approval. She comes swishing over to me with a curt smile, wiping her hands on her smock.

"Hey there, darlin'. Take a seat wherever you'd like. How do you take your coffee?" she chirps.

"Tea, please. Black," I answer.

"You got it, Mr. Jawline. I'll be right back."

She heads to the back kitchen. I scan the diner and find the Pakhan sitting in a booth around the corner from the breakfast counter. It's the only window with the blinds partially open to let the glaring sunset through. The bars of light cut sharply across the older man's face, obscuring his features from a distance. He doesn't flinch at all with the light beaming into his peripheral vision. There's a plate of hashbrowns and a pot of black tea already steaming on the table in front of him. He catches my eye with a pointed glance that pierces right through me. I'm a tough man. I'm not easily ruffled. But the Pakhan has always been able to look straight into my soul, like he can read my mind. It's one of the many traits that make him a formidable, natural leader. I stroll over to his booth.

"Zakhar," he greets me in a low, gruff voice. He gestures to the seat across the table. "Come. Sit. We have much to talk about."

I take my seat as the waitress comes back with another pot of tea and a mug for me. She lights up at the sight of us at one table.

"So nice to see a father and son spending time together," she remarks. "Rare sighting these days."

The Pakhan smiles warmly. With a sparkle in his eye, he answers, "Family comes first above all else, I always say."

She looks positively tickled by his heartfelt response, looking back and forth between us with admiration. "You boys need a menu?" she asks.

I'm about to answer no when the Pakhan speaks up again, "Actually, my boy here is a big fan of steak and eggs. Well done and scrambled." He glances to me for confirmation.

I've never ordered that particular combination in my life, but I quickly smile and nod. I tell her, "That's right."

"You got it, honey," she says, and turns back to the kitchen.

The Pakhan's smile fades a little as he watches to make sure she's out of sight and earshot. Then he leans toward me and says, "I received a very unexpected call on Wednesday evening from a contact of mine with the Coney Island Police. One of my best young Avtoritets is in custody on assault charges, and another one is recovering from said assault. Would you happen to know anything more about that?"

It's a gently-worded question, delivered with the bemused indifference of a much less threatening man. Like he's making small talk instead of interrogating me. But we both know I was there that night.

I look around to make sure the few other customers aren't paying attention. They're all in their own little worlds, and our hushed conversation is covered by the jukebox tunes anyway.

I answer him, "It wasn't supposed to go down like that."

He sips his coffee and chuckles grimly. "No. Certainly not. But now that the smoke has cleared over the past thirty-six hours, I have to wonder… who do I hold responsible for this?"

My jaw tightens. I sit up straighter. I recognize what I must do. As second-in-command to the Pakhan, it is my responsibility to keep the Avtoritets in check, but also to keep them safe. Or at the very least, out of police custody, which could have drastically negative repercussions for the organization as a whole. The Pakhan maintains his cool, detached demeanor, but I know there's anger fizzing under the surface. He wants answers.

"I take full responsibility for what happened," I offer. "Gerasim reached out to me specifically. I didn't hesitate to help him, but I should have done a more thorough job of securing the area before engaging."

He steeples his fingers on the table between us. He fixes me with an unwavering stare. "Now, Gerasim tells me you are *not* to blame. He believes it was his mistake."

"His impulse was correct," I reply. "He suspected Yury of buying drugs with Obshchak funds, tracked him to Coney Island, and set up an opportunity for us to catch Yury in the act."

"And did you?" the Pakhan questions, sitting back.

I nod. "Yes. We both saw him exchanging money for drugs. We tried to follow him, but Yury caught sight of us and bolted, which led to a foot chase."

"And ended with an assault?" he says.

"Gerasim tackled Yury to the ground to restrain him, but Yury had a knife," I relay.

The Pakhan is nodding slowly now, putting the full picture together. "Ah, Yury. I remember the day he was born. Strange, the way time changes everything. I take it he did not go quietly once you and Gerasim cornered him."

"No. And then the police arrived. A civilian must have alerted them to our pursuit. But they weren't the cops we know," I reveal.

"Well, even *I* cannot put every officer on payroll," the Pakhan chuckles. "And I'm sure you understand that, as the primary security force, you should have known about the changing of shifts. You should never have walked through the gates at Luna Park without clearing the mission with one of our guys. You are the thin membrane protecting this organization, and if you can't do that..."

I don't give excuses. I know better than that.

"You're right. I should have been more cautious," I agree.

"Gerasim is a fine Avtoritet. Loyal, devoted, hard-working. Regardless of how it happened, I loathe the thought of him languishing in a jail cell," he points out.

"I promise I'll handle it," I assert.

"You'd better," he says firmly.

The waitress brings over my plate of steak and eggs, arranged to look like two eyes and one large, brown, gaping smile. She seems quite proud of it.

"Wow. Thank you. This looks fantastic," I tell her.

"Thought you two boys might could use a smile," she remarks. "Can I bring you anything else? Ketchup? Steak sauce?"

"Just a to-go box, please," the older man says. "And the check."

The waitress looks slightly disappointed, but shrugs it off. "Of course!" she says, swishing back to the kitchen. The Pakhan starts putting on his jacket and scarf to leave. I do the same. The waitress comes back out with a Styrofoam box and the check.

"You two have a good night, now, alright?" she says.

"Same to you, Miss. Thank you for the splendid service," the Pakhan replies.

He glances out the window, through the slats in the blinds, and makes pointed eye contact with the driver parked just outside. He picks up the to-go box, proceeds to dump the contents of my untouched plate into it, and gives me a wink.

"My dogs will enjoy this meal," he says, sliding the check across the table to me. He adds, "Have a safe evening, Zakhar."

I wait for his shiny BMW to leave the parking lot, then I step out into the cold autumn evening myself. As I climb behind the wheel and fire up the engine, my mind is already back at the safehouse with Hartley. I cannot allow her to become a distraction from my true purpose. The Pakhan is right—it's my job to protect the organization as a whole. I can't do that with half my mind somewhere else. So, if I can't separate the two, and I refuse to let her go, that can mean only one thing.

Hartley must become part of my world. But to see if she is ready, I will have to test her.

CHAPTER 14

HARTLEY

The sun beaming through the windshield feels so warm on my skin, even though it's cold outside. I'm in the passenger seat of my master's black sedan, and he's behind the wheel. We are parked on Surf Avenue in Brooklyn, a street running along the back of Luna Park. In fact, from here I can see the black wrought-iron gates and the twisted track of the Cyclone. On the other side are shops and restaurants bordering on Square Park. I squint into the afternoon sunlight, trying to soak up every bit of imagery I can get. After all, I've been slowly losing my mind, stuck inside that little bedroom with no windows and no exits, and I don't know when I'll be set free like this again.

But I'm not naive enough to think he's giving me a break for my own enjoyment. If he's willing enough to risk my escape like this, it must be for a damn good reason. I look over at him, trying to parse out the intent behind his dark, stoic expression.

"What day is it?" I ask quietly.

"Tuesday," he answers.

I feel jolted by this information. It's been a whole week since he first captured me. On the one hand, a week sounds like an interminable amount of time to be trapped in a two-room suite. On the other hand, so much has changed for me in that time, it seems crazy that only seven days separate me from the life I was leading before. I was Maggie for three months, but a week in my master's grasp has wrung that fake identity out of me. He stripped me down to my core, and I don't know how to be anyone but myself anymore. At least when I'm with him. There's no use hiding from him; he sees everything. He understands me even before I do.

Just hours ago, I woke to the sound of the bedroom door unlocking and clicking open. I sat up in the darkness and heard my master's voice beckoning for me to get dressed and come with him. He laid an outfit on the bed for me and remained in the room, standing there watching me as I followed his commands. I rose, washed, preened, and put on the clothes he brought me.

I'm wearing a black cashmere sweater, dark jeans, high-quality woolly socks, and a pair of killer knee-high black boots. As Master requested, my blonde hair is tied back in a high ponytail. There's a coat of mascara on my lashes and a smudge of tinted lip balm. A glance in the side mirror tells me I look stylishly put-together, definitely *not* like a girl who's been kidnapped and held captive for a week.

"Don't get me wrong, it's nice to be out, but… why are we here?" I pick up the courage to ask him. Master turns that fierce, penetrating gaze on me.

"Remember when I said you'd have to prove yourself trustworthy?" he says.

My heart flutters, recalling that moment. How he made me weak, how he made my pussy gush with pleasure. Honestly, I would have agreed to anything. I swallow hard and nod.

"This is your test," he goes on. "Around the corner from here is a police station. I need you to go inside for me."

My mouth falls open in surprise. "Wh-what?" I stammer. "Why?"

"You must retrieve some evidence they have on a colleague of mine," he explains, like it's not the strangest thing anyone has ever asked of me.

"How do I do that?" I balk. "I don't understand."

"His name is Gerasim Kamenev. He was arrested by mistake. He's innocent, and I need whatever evidence the cops may have on him," he says.

"I don't think they'll give it to me," I falter.

A twinge of a smile touches his lips and disappears. He looks deep in my eyes.

"No. They won't hand it to you," he says. "You will have to steal it."

I almost laugh, I'm so shocked. "Steal? From the police?"

Master isn't laughing. "Yes. That is what we're here to do."

"But… why me? I don't know anything about this stuff. What if I get caught? What do I tell them?" I ask, starting to panic.

He cups my cheek in his hand. I lean into his touch, feeling instantly calmed. His thumb strokes my bottom lip as he murmurs, "You know how to lie. You were pretending to be someone else when I found you. Lying to the whole world, *Maggie.*"

I prickle at the name, but say nothing. He continues, "This relationship is about trust, *malyshka.* Remember, I put my knife to your throat and let you live. You will do this task for me, and I will continue to let you live. In fact, as another token of my trust in you… I will give you *my* true name."

My eyes widen slightly in surprise, a flush coming to my cheeks as he mentions that knife. He twists my soul, the way he talks about something so dangerous, while promising me something so… precious.

He's still an enigma to me, and I know that his name… that's a special gift that I'm certain he doesn't give lightly. And just like him, that gift is as exciting as it is deadly, because knowing it comes with a risk. A pretty big risk.

Kidnappers usually aren't huge on their victims being able to identify them, after all.

"You can trust me," I promise him.

He stares at me a moment longer, a faint smile teasing the corner of his lips.

"My name is Zakhar. But to you, I am Master. I put my life in your hands now. If you behave yourself, I will reward you. However, if you betray me…" he trails off grimly.

He doesn't need to finish the threat. He pulls his hand back, and I have to fight the urge to move towards it.

"Do you understand?" Zakhar questions.

"Yes. I understand," I whisper. "But… they lock the evidence up, right?"

"In your purse you have your picks. I know you can

handle yourself. I wouldn't trust you to do this if I thought I was just handing you over to the law."

I glance at my purse, and slowly I nod. What choice do I have?

"I will circle back for you," he promises. "Now, go."

He all but ushers me out of the car, and drives away down Surf Avenue. I watch the black car disappear around a corner, my heart pounding in my chest. I feel numb with fear as I walk to the end of the block and turn toward the police department. Every car and person that passes makes me more nervous. I feel like everyone is watching me. After a week in that room, the sights and sounds of Brooklyn are overwhelming. I'm almost relieved when I reach the station.

I take a deep breath and walk into the dingy brick building. The security guard pats me down while I avoid eye contact.

"Do you want to walk through or use the wand?"

"Uh, I'll walk through," I decide, and I follow his instructions, putting my purse aside. The lockpicks look like hair pins, but I'm still afraid he'll find them.

I'm distracted as I walk through the metal detector, and I jump when the machine beeps.

"Do you have any metal on? Belt…" He pauses for a second as he looks at the leather collar around my neck, a disapproving shadow passing over his eyes, "jewelry?"

I flush as my hands go to the back of my neck, unfastening the collar and putting it aside. I feel naked without it, but this time, when I walk through again, the machine stays silent.

I take the leather collar back, and instantly go to put it back on.

"My dog has one just like that," he says without a hint of humor to his tone as he hands me back my purse. I can't wait to get away from me, and after signing in, I continue on. All around me, I see cubicles and closed doors, detectives coming and going. There is a constant chorus of ringing phones, fingers typing on keyboards, the scribble of pencil on paper, and hushed conversation. I step up to the receptionist's desk, where a middle-aged woman with purple-rimmed glasses is juggling two phone calls and a stack of paperwork at the same time.

She barely glances at me until I clear my throat and say, "Hi there. I would like to report a crime, please."

The next thing I know, there's a male officer with a bald patch leading me into a private room. My heart is pounding in my ears. My hands are slick with sweat. My thoughts are so jumbled up. What lie do I make up? How do I find the evidence room?

And the biggest question in the back of my mind flares again: should I take this golden opportunity to turn Zakhar in and free myself from captivity for good? I know his name, now. I know enough about him that I could turn him in. And he is a dangerous man.

The detective shuts the door and sits in front of me. "So, what brings you in today, ma'am?" he questions, folding his hands in front of him.

"I-I have information about a crime that was committed. Against me."

"By whom?" he asks.

I feel my face start to burn. I need to be strategic here, but my thoughts are racing, and I'm struggling to find my footing.

"Uh, a man. A man I know," I tell him. "Well, I don't know him very well, actually…"

He takes a pen from behind his ear and clicks it open to start writing on a notepad. "Okay. Go on. What is the man's name?"

It could be over so quickly if I tell the truth. I could escape Zakhar. I could be free! The temptation pulses hot in my mind. Over the course of a week, I must have thought about this a thousand times.

I could go back to my life, the one I had reclaimed. Or, well, I'd probably have to start another new life, somewhere else… Funny how that hadn't occurred to me before.

My fingers trace along the edge of the leather collar as I swallow nervously. What has Zakhar done to me? I spoke the words, pledged myself to him, but now I was having to confront the actual reality of it all.

Of the fact that they weren't just words.

I meant it when I said I wanted to be his. Hot tears spring to my eyes again and my heart races in my chest.

Oh God, I really do have feelings for him.

"Miss? Can you tell me his name?" the cop prompts me.

I bite my lip to stop it from trembling. "I'm having a hard time remembering his name right now," I tell him in a softer, higher voice.

"I thought this man was known to you," he questions.

"He goes by a lot of names," I tell him, trying to be as honest as I can be.

"Well, let's start with one, and we'll go from there."

This is it. I can do it. I can come clean. That's what girls who are kidnapped by possessive men who want to claim them do.

But whenever I open my mouth to try to turn him in, the tears burn hotter in my eyes, until one finally spills. I swipe it away, shocked at how much I'm unravelling.

"I'm sorry. It's just really hard to be here, and… my period just started and I think the, uh, hormones are clouding my memory a little bit." I shift uncomfortably in my seat. "Do you mind if I run to the bathroom?"

He looks pained, but realizes there's no use holding me. He reluctantly stands up to get the door and points me down the hall. "Just down there to the right," he says.

"Thank you. I'm sorry."

I walk down the hallway with a purpose, but take my time. I see the bathroom door to my right. I glance back to make sure nobody is watching, and then I keep going down the hall. Every cell in my body is on high alert, my eyes peeled. I wander around for a few minutes, nodding and smiling at those who pass, trying to look nonchalant. I'm starting to panic when finally, I come across a door marked EVIDENCE ROOM. The door hadn't closed all the way, catching on a ratty rug that had become folded in on itself, and with my heart beating out of my chest, I slip inside.

If literally anyone is in here, I'm done for, and Zakhar's plan falls apart.

He must be desperate to lay this all on me.

I feel a strange rush of pride, knowing how much he trusts me.

Or how expendable I am, my fear prods at the back of my mind.

I don't have time to indulge it.

I'm overwhelmed by the towering shelves of evidence, collected into bags and boxes with case numbers and surnames labeling them. I hear other people moving around a few rows away. I tiptoe through the maze of evidence until, miraculously, I discover a box with the name KAMENEV on it. The date is October 27.

My hands tremble violently as I carefully slide the box out and open the flap to reveal a wad of cash and a cell phone with a cracked screen. I hear footsteps approaching from both directions, and hurriedly stuff the cash inside my left knee-high boot, and the cell phone in the right side. I duck down and move as silently as I can with the uncomfortable bulges against my calves. I wait for the coast to clear and then I bolt for the door.

I'm almost hyperventilating as I shut it behind me and power-walk down the hallway, passing the bathroom. I see the interrogation room with the door ajar, and I tiptoe past.

I can see the front desk now, I'm so close.

Freedom is right there, and Zakhar is waiting for me. Just twenty more steps and I'll be back outside. The cash rubs against my calf, straining against the leather of my boots. I have no idea how much money I'm carrying, but robbing evidence from a police station is definitely something that'll put me in prison.

What the hell am I doing?

Not only am I not turning Zakhar in, but I'm actually taking on a massive risk for him!

I trip up on the edge of the doorway, and catch myself just before I stumble. I'm almost there, and then my heart catches in my throat.

"Excuse me, where do you think you're going?"

CHAPTER 15

ZAKHAR

My hands slide down the leather steering wheel as I turn the car around the corner of Neptune and 12th, avoiding the various chunks of road work. My eyes are narrowed as I peer through the late afternoon glare. The sun is in the most obnoxious position in the sky, making it difficult to see the faces of pedestrians on the sidewalk. Normally, that wouldn't matter much. But right now, it's vitally important that I keep tabs on the crowd coming and going through this area. I am looking for one person in particular: Hartley.

It hasn't been very long, maybe fifteen or twenty minutes since she stepped out of my car and I watched her disappear around the corner. She looked so small and delicate, alone on the sidewalk with that fear in her blue eyes. I hope she was able to hide that fear from the cops, and I suspect she was. I wasn't bluffing when I reminded her that she knows how to lie. I may be able to see right through her, but the rest of the world only sees the pretty facade she puts up. It's what allowed her to survive for so long as Maggie, undetected. If she wants to hide something, she will find a way to do it convincingly.

The only problem is that she might not choose that path. As obedient as she has become through my conditioning, I still don't know for certain that she won't betray me. After all, I've set her up for the most revealing test of her loyalty and character. I sent her straight into the lair of the enemy, looking like a little lost girl in need of rescuing. As the minutes tick by, I grow more nervous.

I should be concerned that she'd turn me in. I did give her my true name, after all, and she has seen more than she should of my life. She could tell the cops enough to find me, let them know she was sent to retrieve the evidence, fucking over Gerasim.

And yet what really worries me is the thought of losing her.

Trusting her with this is risky. Stupid, even. It's not something I'd have ever considered before. But I need to know that she wants to be with me. That she chooses to be with me.

That's why my palms are so sweaty as I grip the steering wheel so tight, my forearms bulging with muscle and veins.

This isn't a game anymore.

It's not even about the sex.

Hartley is everything I've ever wanted or needed in a woman, and now I have to wait to find out if she's really, truly mine.

I circle the block again, taking a slightly more circuitous route this time. I vary my laps to avoid looking suspicious, especially this close to a police station. My years with the Bratva have taught me to blend in and make myself part of the scenery. I have grace under pressure. I'm not afraid of authority. I don't know if I can say the same for Hartley.

Second thoughts cloud my mind. Perhaps it's too early to trust her with this. It's only been just over a week since we reunited, and I've spent more of that time than I'd like running operations away from the safehouse. She borders on a dangerous distraction for me, and I hoped that I could incorporate her into my lifestyle, as a companion. Someone beautiful and obedient, strong but loyal. Someone who can keep up with my demands on the job as well as in the bedroom. I've watched her closely, even before I made my move to finally kidnap her, and come to the conclusion that she has infinite potential.

But the truth of the matter is that I still don't know her that well.

Compared to the years of camaraderie built with many members of the organization, Hartley and I are almost strangers.

Apart from whatever loyalty I've managed to instill in her over the course of one week, she has no real material reason not to turn me in. For all I know, she could be helping the police assemble a task force to take me down right this second. It would be so simple for her to do. It's a straightforward narrative to swallow: a pretty girl in a modest outfit and a leather collar, tearfully recounting how she's been kidnapped and held captive for the dark sexual whims of a mafioso predator.

Hartley and I both know how nuanced it really is—how much she wants it when I touch her, how desperately she aches for me to command her pleasure.

At least, I hope so.

I'm not a man prone to doubting my instincts, but these feelings are all… new. I want her more than anything in the world, and more than that, I want her to want it just as bad.

My car rolls down Surf Avenue to the stoplight. I put on my turn signal and stare down the sidewalk as I approach the police station for another pass. My pulse quickens as my eyes dart from face to face.

"Damn it," I swear softly, not seeing Hartley anywhere. "What's taking so long?"

But then, just as I'm about to pass the entrance to the station, the door swings open and the most beautiful girl in the world steps out onto the street. Her eyes are big and round, her cheeks are flushed, and she's looking around nervously. I slow down and pull to the curb. Hartley's expression shifts from panic to relief when she sees me.

A rush of warm blood pulses through me, and the tension I was holding in my neck eases away. She chose me.

The fires inside me instantly grow hot as I watch her shoulders relax and her eyes soften before she breaks into a jog to get to me.

I push open the passenger door and she slides in, breathing hard. I want to grab her face, press her perfect lips to mine and claim her right then and there, but reason wins out. I kick the car into drive again and pull out onto the street, making a beeline for Brighton Beach now that our Coney Island business is concluded.

"I did it," she blurts out. "I-I found the evidence!"

I can't help it.

I'm impressed. Really fucking impressed.

She definitely has what it would take to be my girl.

I watch her from my peripheral, unzipping her knee-high boots and pulling out two handfuls of evidence. There's a thick stack of cash with a drop of dark red blood dried on it, and a cell phone with a shattered screen. When she clicks the side button, the screen lights up inconsistently and the low battery warning flashes.

"Sorry I took longer than I expected, they gave me a stack of pamphlets and kept telling me all these support numbers before they let me leave," she rambled off, looking exhilarated as she caught her breath. "That was the scariest thing I've done…" she paused, looking up for a moment. "Well, I guess the scariest thing I've done today, at least."

I grin over at her—a true, unrestrained grin. She's beaming back at me with those bright blue eyes and those rosy cheeks all blushing with exhilaration, and I swear, I've never seen a prettier sight in my life.

"You've done well. Put that stuff in the bag on the back seat," I instruct.

She does as she's told, stuffing the cash and cell phone inside an unassuming grocery store tote bag I brought along for this express purpose. It may seem risky to transport evidence in an open bag, but optics are everything. No one would expect to find criminal evidence nonchalantly tossed into a colorful Wegman's bag decorated with illustrations of fresh produce.

"Good girl," I tell her. "Excellent work."

I notice the way she perks up at 'good girl'. She bites her lip and looks at me with those luminous, seductive eyes. I can see the way her hands shake ever so slightly. I hear her breathing, quick and exhilarated. She reaches up to tighten her ponytail and my cock stirs. Immediately, I picture her leaning over my lap with those pretty lips wide open. I don't have to imagine it for long, though, before my perfect little companion makes it a reality.

Almost as though she's questioning if it's okay, she very slowly reaches across the console toward me, staring at my face. I tear my eyes from the road long enough to meet her gaze and give a nod of approval. She licks her lips with anticipation and lets her hand drop to my lap. She begins to massage my bulging cock over my jeans, making me stiffer by the second. Her dainty hand slides up and down my growing shaft while I focus on driving. Hartley unzips my jeans and slips her hand inside, rubbing me through my boxers. The thin fabric only adds a layer of delicious friction to her rhythmic strokes. Once I'm hard as a rock and pulsing with need, she finally slips my cock free through the front of my boxers.

Cars close in around us on either side as we roll through late-afternoon city traffic. I trust the tinted windows to hide us, but I know one very close look would catch us in the act. Instead of detracting, though, the risk of being seen getting road head only intensifies the experience. My core tightens as my beautiful captive bends over to flick her tongue over the swollen tip. She moans, taking me down inch by inch. My jaw goes slack and I have to keep my eyes on the road while Hartley eagerly licks, strokes, and sucks my cock. I gently tug her ponytail now and again to remind her who's in control, but she's drunk on dick. She doesn't care who sees, how messy it gets. Her saliva and my precome glisten on her lips and chin when we stop in front of my apartment in Brighton Beach. I'm so close to coming already, but we're just beginning.

I rush her out of the car and up the steps to my building. I'm tearing off her modest little outfit before the door even shuts all the way behind us. I pull her sweater off and tear the bra from her ribs, making her gasp as her full breasts spill free. I bury my face in her chest, nipping and suckling her nipples to make her tremble with delight. I gather her close in my arms, half-marching and half-carrying my conquest to the loft bedroom. I'm reminded of the first time we were together, when we met that night at the Velvet Kiss Lounge.

Only this time, we aren't strangers anymore. She belongs to me, and now that I know she can be trusted, I don't intend to ever let her go. There's genuine passion when our lips crash together, genuine care when I toss her on the bed and flip her onto her stomach. I tug her boots and jeans off, then bind her ankles to the footboard. Her legs are spread wide open, with her ass up in the air and her face smushing into the bedspread. I tie her wrists together behind her back with a knotted cloth tie. She's clad only in a tight, barely-there lace thong, which reveals the full, delicious bubble of her ass.

I shrug out of my clothes and take my rightful place on the bed, looming over my prey. Hartley looks back at me with those full lips and gorgeous eyes while I smack her ass hard. She whimpers as a red handprint glows angry on her smooth, milky skin. I slide my hand between her ass cheeks and downward over her damp, warm mound. She shivers at the light touch of my fingertips, running across her sensitive clit through the lacy fabric.

I cluck my tongue with mock pity as I tease her clit with two fingers. "So wet for me. Already soaking through your panties," I grunt.

I slip my fingers underneath the crotch of her thong

and she moans when I touch her bare, glistening pussy. I stroke up and down her soft flower, driving her wild with need. She wiggles her ass at me in response, as though begging to be fucked.

But I want to hear it. Out loud.

"Tell me what you want, *malyshka*," I growl.

"I want you," she whimpers.

"Be—more—specific," I command through gritted teeth, punctuating each word with a stroke across her clitoral hood. By now, she's twitching and pulsing around my fingers.

"I want you to fuck me!" she cries out.

"That's right," I grunt. "You *need* my cock inside your pretty cunt."

"I need it," she agrees breathlessly. "Please!

I position my cock at her slick hole, teasing the band of nerves there for a moment before I shove my full, throbbing length inside of her in one powerful motion. Hartley yelps in mingled pain and pleasure, and I grasp her hips so tightly my fingernails dig into her luscious flesh. I rear back and pound into her, hard enough to make her ass jiggle. I pull almost fully out, then spear into her again. She's moaning and dripping around my cock when I grab her ponytail and tilt her head back. She's completely paralyzed between the ankle restraints, wrist tie, and her hair wrapped up in my fist.

But like a good, obedient slut, she gives herself over to my control. She doesn't fight my authority in the least; in fact, she encourages me by squeezing her pelvic muscles tight around my cock, making me see stars. I look down at her, bent and twisted in my grip, sweating and leaking tears of filthy ecstasy. I smack her ass, pull her hair, and pound her pussy so hard I know she'll be aching for days.

"Who owns this sweet little hole?" I grunt.

"You," she purrs between loud, wet smacks of my cock in her cunt.

"Who makes you come harder than you ever have?" I hiss.

"You do!" she gasps, her thighs starting to shake.

"*Da*, my pet," I groan as my own pleasure reaches a fever pitch. "And I want you to come for me, Hartley. Come for your master. Now."

"Ohhhh," she wails.

Her body goes rigid, then limp through wave after wave of climax. I feel her tighten around my thick cock. She clenches again and again, pushing me to the edge, too. Her body is twitching and gleaming with sweat. Tears shine on her cheeks, and her once-flouncy ponytail is now a messy blob. I pump her full of my come, emptying every last drop deep inside her womb. I want to fill her completely, make it so that no one else can ever claim her.

I lean over her bent body and kiss her cheek, her hair, her forehead. I gently tug her hair free from the ponytail and run my fingers through it. I caress her, whisper soft words to her in Russian I know she can't understand. I'm so proud of my little captive. Not only has she proved herself a worthy companion in the streets, but I know without a shred of doubt that she is my perfect match in the bedroom. She doesn't fight my strength. She accepts that I am in control. She revels in her helplessness and climaxes on command.

"You're a fast learner," I compliment her as I free her wrists.

She folds her arms under her head, looking back at me with a soft smile.

"You have so much to teach me," she replies.

"Yes," I agree. "I do."

Suddenly, our passionate bliss is interrupted by a sharp knock at my front door downstairs from the loft.

"What is that?" she asks worriedly. I don't answer.

I withdraw from her and hastily pull on my jeans. My mind shifts from sensual to aggressive mode, and my training kicks in. Leaving her on the bed, sticky with my seed, I march down the stairs. I don't know what will be waiting for me, friend or foe.

But I know one thing for certain: Hartley belongs utterly to me now, and I will defend what's mine to the death.

CHAPTER 16

HARTLEY

My body is rigid as I lie on my stomach, my back and ass exposed to whoever might come barging into the room. I'm still stunned at how quickly our sensual scene shifted into something totally different. Zakhar went from buried inside my pussy to rushing out the door within seconds when we first heard that knock. He seems to have recovered more quickly than I can, as I'm still breathing hard and coming down from the overpowering orgasm Master gave me. I feel my legs trembling and my pussy clenching over and over again. My slick honey drips down my inner thighs, staining Zakhar's bedsheets. My heart is pounding, my head dizzy. The bedroom smells like sex.

But as the endorphins simmer down, I start to feel my muscles aching, a delayed reaction to our forceful love-making. The fuzzy halo of warmth that clouded my mind ebbs away to reveal the same underlying sense of paranoia I had before. I'm coming back to reality now, and fear trickles into my veins. It occurs to me that we aren't at the safehouse where Zakhar kept me this past week, we're at his own place. Which probably equates to less privacy, less security. At the safehouse, maybe I was a captive, but I was at least pretty certain that Zakhar could keep me protected there. I was at his mercy, but *only* his. Even the one time I did hear evidence of another man being in the safehouse briefly, the stranger didn't interact with me at all. I was Zakhar's perfectly kept little secret.

Here, though… I don't know how safe I am.

In fact, I don't even know if Zakhar is safe, either.

I strain my ears as hard as I can, even shutting my eyes to try and focus fully on what I can hear. But try as I might, I can't really tell what's going on out there. All I can detect are muffled voices, seemingly of a lower pitch, so I assume it must be Zakhar and some other man. Maybe more than one. The tone of their voices doesn't alert any red flags for me; it doesn't sound like they're arguing. More like a terse discussion. The words, though, are way beyond my comprehension. I can't even tell they're speaking English.

My nerves start to get to me. It hits me how vulnerable I am like this, with my ankles bound to the footboard. My hands are free, but it takes a little maneuvering for me to wiggle backward on my stomach and slowly bring my legs closer together. Once I'm close enough to the end of the bed, I manage to pull myself up on my knees and look back at the cuffs binding my ankles. It's annoying, just far enough back for it to be a pain twisting around, trying to pick at the cuffs. Of course, it doesn't help that my hands are shaking like a leaf. I bite my lip, getting frustrated with myself as my twitchy fingers fail again and again to free my ankles. My heartbeat picks up as my panic grows. I start breathing hard and fast while my fingers slip uselessly around the knots.

Where is Zakhar? Is he alright? Is he coming back for me?

Fear runs cold through my body as I imagine my handsome, strong master lying dead on the street in a pool of blood. It's a horrific image that brings hot tears to my eyes, made worse by the realization that nobody knows I'm here other than Zakhar. If something happens to him, I could be trapped here, left to waste away with my legs bound to the bed.

"Please come back," I murmur tearfully.

Almost as though he could hear my plea, I hear the distinctive thud of the front door closing downstairs. I perk up at the sound of familiar footsteps thumping quickly up the stairs. He's running, taking the stairs two at a time to get to me faster. I watch the top of the steps with wide eyes, craving his presence. Relief washes over me when Zakhar comes hurtling onto the loft level, coming right toward me. There's a grim expression on his face. His dark eyes are steely, his jaw tight. He goes straight to the footboard and hastily releases me from my shackles.

"What's going on? Who was that?" I question.

As soon as my ankles are free, I turn over to sit on my butt, watching Zakhar rush to the closet to grab a big, fleece-lined jacket. He also scoops up my jeans and sweater, tossing them on the bed along with the jacket, a pair of socks, and the knee-high boots I wore to the station.

"Come on. Get dressed. We have to go," he commands in a low, controlled voice.

"Where are we going?" I ask.

He doesn't reply. I slide off the bed and start hurriedly

putting on clothes. Zakhar puts a big jacket on, too, after checking the interior pockets for… something. As I'm pulling on my boots, he looks at his watch.

"Hartley. We have to leave now," he urges me. There's a warning in his eyes.

"Okay, okay!" I mutter, getting to my feet.

Zakhar reaches for my hand and drags me out of the bedroom. I can hardly keep up with him when we hit the stairs. It's freezing cold when we step outside. The temperature has dropped considerably since the sun went down, and I'm momentarily knocked back by the gust of frigid air on my face. I'm still trying to catch my breath when Zakhar opens the passenger door of his car and basically shoves me inside. I click my seatbelt as he jumps behind the wheel and throws the car into drive.

I look around in the darkness, searching the streets for any sign of trouble. I don't see the man Zakhar was talking to earlier. In fact, the street looks almost unnaturally empty. I look at the digital time on the dashboard. It's barely seven o'clock in the evening—prime time for people coming home from work or getting ready to go out for the night. But there's not a soul to be found, even when we turn the corner down another street.

"It's so quiet," I murmur to myself in confusion.

Like the streets have been cleared out. Like everyone is inside, hiding. But from what? I turn back to Zakhar, hoping for some response. But he's fully focused on the road in front of him. His dark eyes are narrowed, his knuckles white on the steering wheel.

"Zakhar," I say out loud for the first time.

He glances at me. "What is it?" he asks.

I heave a sigh. "We got out of there in a big hurry. Why can't you tell me what's happening? I'm scared," I admit.

"Need-to-know basis," he answers gruffly.

"Seriously? Please! At least, tell me where you're taking me!" I blurt out.

"I'm taking you to my mother," he says, looking back to the road.

My jaw drops. "Wh-what?" I splutter. "Your mom? Is this really the time to do the whole 'meet your parents' thing?"

"You will be safe there," my master explains. "Saf*er.*"

"Safe from what? I don't understand," I continue.

"It's not for you to understand right now," he dismisses me.

I sink back into the seat, arms crossed over my chest. We turn down Brighton 6th Street, rolling through blocks of modest townhouses and apartments. In the darkness I can barely make out the ads for small Russian grocery stores, an in-home daycare, and a sign offering bridge classes. It would be a cute, cozy little neighborhood in the warm light of day. But now, the streets are oddly dim, with even the OPEN signs turned off. Nobody is on the sidewalk. Zakhar and I might as well be the only people left alive. It's so eerie.

"Does this have anything to do with our trip to the police station today?" I press him. "Please, just talk to me."

"We're here," Zakhar answers.

The car comes to a stop in front of a townhouse building with white siding on the top and rusty red brick on the bottom. It looks to be two stories plus a basement suite, with a few shallow steps leading to the front door. There's a yard in front with a fence and a tiny vegetable garden and a single lawn chair facing the street. Narrow alleyways separate the building from the nearly identical ones on either side. As I step out of the car and breathe in deeply, I pick up the faint brine of the sea rolling in, and realize we must only be a few blocks over from the coast.

I don't get much time to contemplate, though, because Zakhar drags me up the steps in a hurry. He fishes a key out of one of his interior jacket pockets and fits it into the lock. It clicks open and he ushers me into the warm, inviting foyer of a small, old townhome. As soon as we're inside, I pick up the scent of spicy black tea and something else… pickles, maybe?

All around, the place looks unquestionably like the residence of an older woman. The sheer number of doilies and framed black-and-white photographs on the walls are proof of that. Every piece of furniture looks at least twenty years old and a little dusty. The floors are thickly carpeted, with intricate rugs everywhere. The shelves are covered in little tchotchkes. There's a set of playing cards on the coffee table next to a crossword puzzle and pencil.

"*Matushka*," Zakhar calls down a hallway.

"Ah, Zakhar!" comes the soft reply.

A small, slightly bent older woman with steel-gray hair pulled into a tight, spiral bun comes shuffling into the foyer. She looks me up and down with a surprisingly shrewd gaze.

"*Eto kto?*" she asks, gesturing to me.

"This is Hartley. I need you to stay with her while I run an errand, *da?*" he says.

His mother fixes me with a piercing gaze and nods slowly. "*Da*. Sit down," she says, nudging me toward the floral couch. "I will make tea."

She shuffles slowly back toward the kitchen. Zakhar looks at me and says, "Stay. You'll be safe here. I'll come back for you when I can."

"No, no, no. Please. Don't leave me," I beg him, starting to freak out.

I make a grab for his hand but he pulls away.

"I will be back soon," he says emphatically.

He opens the door and steps outside. I start to get up and follow him, but then I falter. Despite how badly I want to go with him, I can't disobey. I sit on the edge of the couch, listening to the tea kettle whistling down the hall. I can't stop fidgeting and jiggling my legs. My heart is racing and I feel nauseated. All I want is for Zakhar to come back through that door.

But the next thing I hear chills me to the bone.

A gunshot. Right outside.

Chapter 17

Zakhar

Smoke rises in slow curls through the darkness. It catches the eerie glow of moonlight as I hold the gun straight out, my hand still wrapped around the holster. My finger eases off the trigger only now that the barrel has released. The physical effort of fighting the recoil has my muscles tight with tension. My ears are still ringing from the deafening crack of gunfire. The world is a muffled, dark place while my mind comes back to reality.

The residential street is unnaturally quiet and empty, with not a neighbor or drifter in sight. It's a testament to how accustomed the neighborhood is to strange, frightening occurrences. Not even the sure sound of gunshot on an early Tuesday evening can drag these people out of their houses. It's not just fear that keeps them safe behind their locked front doors—they know better. The vast majority of the inhabitants here are in with the organization, whether formally or informally. They know they receive a modicum of protection or neutrality in exchange for their silence. They don't have to be fully complicit, just quiet.

I lower my gun and take a few measured steps closer. I watch the blood start to stain the front of the young man's sweatshirt, pooling from inside, right over his heart. Judging by his low-quality university sweatshirt and scrawny frame, I can assume this is a lower-ranked member of the brotherhood. A Bratok, meant to fall in line behind his assigned Avtoritet. He's probably never felt powerful in his life before tonight, with that gun in his hand. I feel a twinge of pity for the kid, but it's a fleeting sensation. I did what I had to do. I've done it before, and I know I will have to do it again. There's no point agonizing over my decision to take a man's life this evening. At the end of the day, a Brodyaga is the responsibility of his respective Avtoritet. Clearly, whoever this man belongs to did not have his best interests in mind. The Avtoritet must have known he was sending his Bratok into a dangerous, almost certainly fatal situation.

Either the Avtoritet is callous enough to know the risk and send him anyway or foolish enough not to expect the risk in the first place. Avtoritets are supposed to display better planning than this, and they are definitely not supposed to send their Brodyaga after a higher-ranked member like me. Somebody screwed up big time tonight, and this dead body in front of me is just one piece of the puzzle dropped on my doorstep earlier.

I never expected this evening to take such a dark turn. I was prepared for a long night of claiming my prize, making my pretty little captive come again and again. But the second I heard that knock at my apartment door, I knew my plans were ruined. I immediately understood that this is a potentially dangerous situation. Mafia members know better than to simply show up at my personal, private residence and knock on the door. I am an important man. One does not just casually drop in on the second-ranked man in the org. We have a careful system. We plan ahead of time. We move in secrecy. It's a major sign of disrespect to show up at my door unannounced, not to mention a threat to the security of the entire brotherhood.

It's not that I'm impossible to find; I don't try that hard to conceal my private life. I normally don't have to. Everyone knows the rules. Everyone knows not to try me.

Except for the few scattered civilians who are oblivious (willingly or not) to the mafia presence sinking into every nook and cranny of the city. When I opened my door earlier, I found one of my neighbors standing there. He's a blue-collar worker in his forties or fifties who lives next door. He knocked on my door to confront me about letting 'my friends' park illegally on our street, though of course he shrank back down to size once I opened the door. As soon as his eyes rolled upward to see me towering over him, the guy's angry expression softened a little. He took a step back and put up his hands in surrender, even before I said a word.

The guy said in a gruff voice, "Now, look, I don't want any trouble. But my wife has been pestering me all day to say something about your buddy parking outside our house. I know parking is a bitch, but he can't just block my yard like that. Especially if he's just going to sit in his car talking on the phone from morning 'til night."

So someone has been watching my place all day. I know instantly this is trouble.

Not wanting to give anything away, I kept my voice calm when I replied, "I appreciate your wife's concern. I will deal with the issue right away. Could you point me in the direction of the car so I can speak to my… friend?"

"It's the same one that's been here all day. That silver shitkicker down the block," the neighbor pointed out to me. "Hey… wait!"

As he was pointing to a beat-up silver hatchback with heavily tinted windows, the car's headlights turn on and off. The tires squeal as the car backs out and takes off around the corner. My jaw tightens and my hands close into fists.

"I swear, he's been here all day," my neighbor said helplessly.

"I believe you," I told him. "Don't worry. I'll take care of it."

I shut the door on him. The poor man had no idea of the actual drama and danger unfolding around him; he just thought he was being a hero. But his little neighborhood watch patrol gives me the tip-off I need. Only fellow mafia members would know how to even track me down, and if the Pakhan had authorized a stakeout on my street, I would know about it. The Pakhan trusts me to run my own territory. If he didn't authorize it, then somebody else did.

And if they've been skulking around all day, only a true fumble would make them abandon post. A fumble such as being spotted by the very man he's staking out, perhaps. That's why the silver hatchback took off as soon as my neighbor pointed him out to me. He must have known he was caught. Yet, something told me he wasn't finished yet. In my mind, the guy had to be there for one of two reasons: to catch me in the act with Hartley or to kill me outright.

If I was at the apartment alone, I would have hunkered down with my gun and simply waited for my sloppy stalker to make his move. But I don't walk alone anymore. I have someone else to worry about: Hartley. My apartment was compromised, and since I didn't know who was tailing us, I could no longer trust the mafia safehouses either.

So I headed back upstairs, grabbed Hartley, and immediately headed to my mother's townhouse apartment just a few minutes away. Her place is deeply buried in mafia-controlled Brighton Beach, surrounded by a mix of secure members and civilians in the know. The neighborhood is quiet, uninteresting to police and criminals alike. I assumed we would be safer here. We could lie low until the night passes, at least.

But to my dismay, I notice the silver hatchback in a glint of moonlight when I glance in the overhead mirror. He's only a few blocks behind us as my black sedan pulled in front of my mother's townhouse. He followed us, and now it's too late to try a different location. I had to make a split-second decision in that moment, ignoring Hartley's pleas for an explanation. I had no better option than to hurry her into the house and try to defend this new location… while the two women I care about more than anything else in the world wait innocently inside.

Mere seconds after leaving Hartley in the foyer, I was back outside, ready to confront our pursuant. As I stepped into the night air, I saw him. The young man rushing up from his hastily-parked car along the sidewalk. His body language is clear: slightly bent, arms pumping, his hood up over his head, and his gun ready in his hand. But I see the way he startles and stumbles to a stop when he sees me.

Evidently, he was not expecting me to come out and meet him so aggressively. He must not know me very well… or at all. Perhaps his Avtoritet did not inform him. My main role within the organization is to maintain security, and I don't hesitate to protect what's mine.

The guy makes a move to run for it, then seems to remember his mission. He stops short and raises the gun in the middle of the residential street, aiming right at me.

He says in a shaky voice, "Just obeying orders, man."

But before he can pull the trigger, I lift my gun and fire. The ringing in my ears fades as I look down at my fallen target in his flimsy sweatshirt stained with his own blood. I nudge the hoodie back from his forehead with the tip of my shoe. I don't know the young man's name, but I recognize his face. Part of my position involves memorizing the images of my fellow mafia members, even if I don't take the time to meet them personally. I have to know who answers to whom, and I can tell right off the bat that this Bratok doesn't belong to Gerasim, Arseny, or even Yury. He's assigned to an Avtoritet named Evgeny, a man I've had little to no contact with.

That sneaking suspicion grows stronger in my mind as I peer down at the dead Bratok. Between the Coney Island fiasco and tonight's events, I know something fishy is going on. If Yury isn't the one who authorized him, then he must not be the mastermind. He is probably just another pawn for the real player. As to the game? Only someone ranked as high or higher than Yury could pull this off. Someone who wanted to take out as many

Avtoritets at a time as possible. As the youngest and weakest Avtoritet, Yury is a convenient first domino to knock over. I think about it—Yury and Gerasim were taken down at Coney Island. One set up to buy drugs and betray the brotherhood, the other set up to confront him. Both taken in by the police, which just so happened to be the cops not on our payroll. Two birds, one stone. And now tonight, someone has tried to take me out too.

Clearly, someone is eliminating Avtoritets to try and move up through the ranks. It is my duty to make sure he doesn't complete his mission, but right now, I have a mess on my hands. Luckily, I'm virtually surrounded by allies here. I make a quick phone call and, within minutes, two of my former Bratok roll up to help. Pavel and Timur were my most loyal men when I was still just an Avtoritet myself. I know I can rely on them.

They pull up in Timur's car, already dressed for a dirty job. With the moon shining down on us, we carefully lift the dead Bratok from the pavement and put him in the trunk of Timur's vehicle. Meanwhile, Pavel cleans out the dead man's pockets. We put the dead man's phone, wallet, and gun in the back seat of his car. Pavel slides the bloodied keys into the ignition, and Timur does the same in his own car.

"You know where to go?" I ask them, standing on the sidewalk.

Timur gives me a nod. "The landfill down the coast," he answers grimly.

Pavel leans out the window and says, "And I'll take his belongings back to Yonkers with his car so the cops track him back to his own neighborhood. They won't suspect anything for a good while."

"Excellent. Good work, my old friends," I tell them both.

"You can always count on us. Once a Bratok, always a Bratok," Pavel says.

Timur adds, "Whatever is going on tonight, we're on your side."

Something about his wording seems off. I frown at him. "Is there more?" I question.

He looks surprised to know something I don't. He replies, "I thought you knew. It could be a bunch of stupid rumors, but there's talk about something big going down at the Pakhan's party tonight. I figured this was part of it."

I nod, taking in the information. I tap the tops of each car and say, "Good. Go on."

I watch the cars go in opposite directions, certain that my men will do right. But I see now that tonight's events are just ramping up. I have work to do.

But just as I'm turning back to go inside, I see a flash of movement across my mother's front yard. My hand goes straight to my gun, and then I realize the figure isn't moving toward the front door, but away. Running off down the block.

My heart thuds painfully over a missed beat. In the darkness, my eyes slowly adjust, and I make out the shape of my beloved captive trying to flee from me… again.

CHAPTER 18

HARTLEY

That gunshot flipped a switch inside of me.

The unmistakable crack of gunfire through the air rattled my body. Cold swept over me, then heat. My hands grew clammy and began to shake. In the wake of the gunshot, my ears are ringing. The world is going soft and blurry all around me. Reality is frayed, and suddenly I'm riveted to the spot. A million horrible images flood my mind all at once—pictures of Zakhar lying on the sidewalk with a puddle of blood pooling underneath his twitching body. I imagine his dark eyes wide with fear for the first time, probably ever. Tears prickling in his eyes and mine as the light slowly leaves them. My lip quivers. My eyes sting. Awful conclusions pass through my brain in a frenzy, like the world's most agonizing montage.

What if Zakhar is hurt, and I'm in here hiding like a rat? Maybe he's still alive. Maybe he's only injured, and I could still save him if I'm fast enough.

Through my panic, I hear soft footsteps and the rattling of porcelain dishes behind me. I whirl around to see

Zakhar's mother carefully carrying a tray. There's a little blue teapot with steam drifting from the spout, bringing a gentle spice to the air. She has two teacups, a cream saucer, and some pickle sandwiches with the crust cut off. She looks at me with wise eyes and a somewhat hesitant smile, like she wants to trust me, but she can't be certain. I realize she either didn't hear the gunshot or maybe she's so used to hearing it, she doesn't care. Maybe it just hasn't dawned on her yet that her own son could be the one wearing that bullet.

She's shuffling toward the floral couch and coffee table to set down the tray. For a moment, I feel a lurch of longing. It has been a long time since someone sat me down and offered me tea. Zakhar's mother has such a quiet, calming energy, a tiny part of me aches to sit and sip tea with her. I could pretend for a precious little while that she's someone who loves me. I could act out the fantasy of being cared for. After everything I've been through, that little girl inside of me still craves a sense of belonging. A family. A break from the stress and pain.

I was never safe growing up. My father pretended that he was protecting me from the dangers of the outside world, but he was the one that was putting us all at risk.

When you're dealing in drugs and guns, it's not just the police you have to be on the lookout for. Rival dealers, clients, thieves… There was always a reason to be looking over your shoulder, and keeping people at arms-length. That chatty person at the bus stop might just be trying to learn your schedule, find a weakness in your security.

I had no family. I had no friends.

I've been all alone for so long, and the first time I ever feel safe, and it's with a killer.

I don't know if we found each other by fate or chance, but somehow, we are the missing piece in each other's lives.

I can't let him die out there alone.

So, against his explicit instructions, I turn and dart to the door. Zakhar's mother calls out to me, but I rush out into the night air. The cold momentarily knocks the wind from my lungs, and I waver on the front step, trying to let my eyes adjust to the dark. My stomach is twisting into knots as I make my way down the steps and across the yard. I turn my head back and forth, eyes wide as I search for Zakhar. The street is eerily quiet and empty. It feels almost apocalyptic, like I'm the last person left alive. But then I see movement down a block or so, and my heart skips a beat as I recognize the hulking figure of Zakhar. He's standing up, facing away from me, and barely illuminated in the glow of a car's headlights.

I get a rush of relief that he's okay—or at least upright, not sprawled on the ground in a pool of blood. But no sooner does that thought cross my mind than I flick my gaze downward, and I start to make out the shape of a body on the ground at Zakhar's feet. The body looks limp, but it's moving somehow. It takes another half-second for me to realize that someone else is dragging the body away into an open car. In the road beside that car is another, already pulling away down the street in the opposite direction. I don't understand what is going on. My mind tries to make sense of what I'm seeing, but it won't compute. Surely Zakhar didn't kill that man. Surely, he isn't the bad guy in this situation.

Then I see it—the gun in his hand. As the car door shuts and the second vehicle starts to pull away, Zakhar puts the gun back into his jacket. My heart is pounding. I feel sick. With shaking hands, I reach for the gate at the edge of the front yard. It makes a whiny creaking noise when I open it, and Zakhar spins around, his hand in his jacket like he's about to pull his firearm again—with almost no hesitation. As soon as I see my master's gun pointed at me, the doubts I've been holding back come rushing through my head. That old paranoia sneaks back in, making awful assumptions. Maybe I have this all wrong. Maybe Zakhar isn't keeping me safe from someone else… maybe *he* is the dangerous one.

Details click into place. He must have taken me to that police station to collect evidence to cover his own tracks. He's a criminal, at the *very least* capable of kidnapping a woman off the streets and holding her as a hostage to his own sexual depravity. Now he's potentially a murderer, and I'm a fool for ever trusting him.

As much as it pains me, I know I can't stay here. Even if it's futile, even if he'll catch me, I have to try and make a run for it. Right now. So, with one last tearful gaze at the man who has shown me pleasure I never dreamed of, I bolt down the street. My chest aches with sobs as I pump my arms and legs, pushing myself as fast as I can go. My knee-high boots aren't the best running shoes, but I book it at top speed, knowing I have a true predator on my heels. I run like my life depends on it. Like every enemy I've ever feared is right behind me. I don't let myself look back, for fear I might lose my nerve and go running back to him.

All I hear are my own pounding footsteps, my ragged breathing, and my heartbeat rushing in my ears. Through tear-filled eyes I see a dark vehicle light up and vroom to life just several yards ahead of me. My panicked mind tells me this is my chance—whoever is driving that car might just be my only ticket out of here. I'm running full-tilt in that direction when someone steps out of the passenger side and comes rushing to the sidewalk. A tall man in a long black coat and a beanie appears like a blockade, and within seconds, I'm colliding with his enormous frame. I hit him like a brick wall and again, the air is knocked out of me. I don't even get to recover before his big arms close around me in a tight vise. Too tight—not like he's protecting me, but like he's restraining me. He grunts and lifts me clear off the ground, already rushing back to the car.

I realize instantly that I've made a grave mistake. I start screaming and kicking like crazy, trying to fight back as the mystery man flings open the back seat and starts pushing me inside. I bite and claw at him. I stretch out my arms and legs to make myself too big to fit through the door. I'm so angry—at the world, at this man, at Zakhar, and most of all, at myself. I used to think I was strong and smart. A capable young woman doing her best to escape a dark past I didn't set into motion. But in the arms of a powerful man, I am helpless. Just like I couldn't stand up to Zakhar, I can't fight this man off either. I'm doomed to repeat the same fate.

Over the man's shoulder, I see Zakhar running toward us. He's only ten or so feet away when he skids to a stop and whips out his gun. Aiming it straight at the mystery man, Zakhar shouts hoarsely, "Stop! Let her go or I'll blow your fucking head off!"

But instead of reacting with fear, the man simply cackles and whirls around to face Zakhar, holding me in front of himself like a human shield. His fingernails dig into my wrists as he holds my hands behind my back. I can feel his body heat and smell his rancid breath. I freeze up as cold metal pokes into my temple. He's holding a gun to my head.

"One step closer and I will gladly spill your little whore's brains all over the sidewalk," the kidnapper hisses cruelly. "A mess even you can't clean up."

Zakhar's jaw tightens. He clicks the trigger, but doesn't pull it. I see the pain in his eyes. It's killing him to let me go. But he won't risk my life further. He lowers the gun, giving my captor a withering, hateful glare. A look that promises payback. Maybe not now, but someday.

The man holding me cackles again. "That's what I thought. Enjoy your evening, Alexeyev," he growls. Still pressing the gun to my head, he shoves me into the car. I scream and beat on the window as tears stream down my face. The kidnapper jumps into the passenger seat and shouts, "Go, go, go!"

The driver, a glum-looking man with a scar across his face, throws the car into gear. The vehicle roars off down the street while I desperately watch Zakhar's figure get smaller and smaller. The last thing I see is him turning and running back toward his mother's house. I don't know if he's coming after us or not. But I do know that I've fucked up. I let my old trauma keep me from trusting Zakhar. I let myself be tricked again. I gaze out the window at the dark houses passing by, barely lit by the occasional streetlamp. The driver doesn't say a word as he maneuvers the car out of the neighborhood and eastward to the back streets.

In the passenger seat, my new captor is downright gleeful. He slaps his leg, laughing his ass off as he recounts his success to the unswayed chauffeur.

"Did you see the look on Alexeyev's face? Finally, that bastard gets a taste of his own medicine. Must be torture to watch me drive off with his little pet," he sneers.

The driver glances at me in the rearview mirror. I look back at him tearfully. He doesn't show a lick of regret or remorse. He looks back to the road while his companion continues to talk a big game in the passenger seat.

"Second in command to the Pakhan," he spits with disgust. "As if he's done anything to earn the damn position. A good soldier, maybe, but who cares about 'good'? If we're going to operate outside the law, we might as well get something out of it. Why break the law just to follow stupid rules?"

I listen intently while my heart races.

"Being an Avtoritet used to come with perks, you know. A whole team of Brodyaga at my disposal, the ear of the Pakhan, the trust of our community. That's nice and all, but I can't spend goodwill. Ever since Alexeyev took over security, things have been too clean around here," he reveals. "Impossible to take what's mine with a damn dragon guarding the hoard."

"What?" I murmur barely audibly. It dawns on me that Alexeyev must be Zakhar's surname. This man is specifically talking about him.

"But soon enough, things will be in my favor again. Everything is falling into place just as I planned. All Yury needed was a nudge in the wrong direction. That stupid kid didn't think twice about the money or the drugs. Gerasim took the bait like a good little lapdog. I hoped my anonymous call to the Coney Island cops would bring Zakhar down along with him, but I'll get him in the end," he boasts smugly. "And once I rattle the Pakhan's trust in him, he's done for. You know it's better to be dead than disgraced in the brotherhood," he adds to the driver.

The brotherhood? Yury and Gerasim… a call.

My jaw drops as the realization sets in. This man is the one who set up Zakhar's colleague. Zakhar sent me into the police station for that evidence so he could protect his friend, not so I could hinder an investigation on *him*. I flash back to my childhood, to the feeling of confusion at the whispers all around me. I remember feeling so helpless, surrounded by a complex world I didn't understand, that nobody stopped to explain to me. I feel that way now, like a naive, lost little girl. I'm always running from something, and I always run the wrong way.

"With the Obshchak out of the way, I'll be free to take whatever I want and none will be the wiser. Who will rat me out? Yury? The boy will be lucky to escape the Pakhan's judgment with his life. He's weak. He won't stand up against me, not after he so willingly accepted that cash for drugs. If Zakhar knows what's good for him, he'll back off, too. Disappear into the margins and never show his face here again."

"That will never happen," I blurt out, surprised at my own bravery.

The man scoffs. "He must have done a real number on you to make you trust a man like him. If there's one thing I have to admire about the guy, it's how he's trained you. He has you brainwashed. He doesn't care about you. You're just a sex toy to him. But I bet you miss him like a lover, don't you, stupid girl?"

Tears burn in my eyes again. I clench my fists.

"It will be the greatest pleasure to reform you to my

own tastes," he leers. "The first of many, many things I will take away from Alexeyev."

"I would rather die," I fling back at him angrily.

He whips around in his seat, pointing that gun at me again with a frightening wildness in his gaze. I feel the warmth drain from my face and I fall silent. He grins at my terror.

"There's time enough for both," he threatens darkly.

At just that moment, there's the squeal of tires, and something massive strikes the car with such force that it goes careening in a chaotic circle. In the darkness, I can't make head or tail of what's going on. I hear the men shouting, the driver swearing as he fights to control the vehicle. On the icy road, the car spins around at high velocity. The g-force pushes me into the back of the seat and I shut my eyes tight as the world spins violently around me, and I brace for the inevitable impact that will kill us all.

CHAPTER 19

ZAKHAR

Seeing another man drag Hartley away from me was one of the deepest wounds I have ever suffered. Realizing that that man is not just any garden variety creep, but a powerful and connected Avtoritet was almost worse. I have spent a long time in the underworld of mafia business, and it takes a lot to rattle me. But Hartley isn't from this reality. Any pain or fear she may have suffered at my hands will pale in comparison to whatever Evgeny has planned for her. I am a dangerous man, but I have no desire to hurt her—at least, not without pleasure coming along with it. I can't tell what Evgeny wants with her. Naturally, about a million horrific reasons have occurred to me in the blink of an eye it took for him to haul Hartley off. My blood boils as my rage builds higher and higher. Every second I'm without her feels like a stab to my very soul.

And when that bastard held his gun to her pretty head… well, I've never felt dread like that before. Even in the darkest hour of my bloodiest mission, I maintain my composure. Pain, torture, gore, and death follow me like ugly ghosts. I've made peace with them by now. I know how to stare down a gun barrel without flinching. I don't fear my own death even when it's hot on my heels. Losing friends, brothers in arms, even family—it's part of the life-style I must live.

But Hartley is the exception. She is the one desire that surfaces above the rest. I don't know what caused her to run away from me again. Fear? Panic? Regret? Perhaps she was only confused, surrounded by all these frightening things that don't make sense to her. I am one of those frightening things, to be sure, but we've built so much together already in the short time we've known one another. Watching her disappear down the road, carried off by predators for God knows what purpose, put a lot of things into perspective for me. As that getaway car drove off, it took my heart with it, sitting in the backseat.

As I bolted to my own car and dove behind the wheel, my only thought was to catch up to them, to retrieve her. I can't be apart from Hartley. I need her with me, and not just for her safety. We're meant to be together. I see it clearly now, on the brink of losing her.

It's dark outside. Snow has started to flurry past my windows, obscuring my visibility even more. But it's not vision so much that guides me as I chase down Evgeny's vehicle—it's pure animalistic instinct. I throw caution to the wind. I don't care if I get hurt. I hardly care if I die, except that my death would probably spell out Hartley's death, too. The streets are quiet, and I weave through what little traffic I encounter with precision. I run stop signs and red lights. I floor the gas. I grit my teeth and clench the steering wheel tightly as my car approaches the other from behind on a country road heading east across Long Island. I keep back at first with my lights off to preserve the element of surprise. And when I see my opportunity, just the two vehicles alone on the stretch of road, I take it.

I shove my foot down on the gas pedal. The engine roars as my car goes shooting ahead of the other vehicle. The driver doesn't even have time to react before I jerk the wheel and slam into the front passenger side, where I know Evgeny is sitting. There's an earth-shattering crash and screech of metal on metal as my car pounds the other off the road. With the snow settling into ice on the road, the vehicle goes careening in a violent spin. My own car ricochets from the impact, spinning in the opposite direction. There are a few seconds of near-weightlessness before my tires hit a patch of piled snow and crunches to a stop.

I'm disoriented as I climb out of the car and run toward the other vehicle… which has crashed into a tree. My first and only thought is: *Hartley.* I run faster than I ever have through the snow falling heavier and the smoke in the air. In the dark, I can hardly tell I'm going the right way except for the flickering tail lights. My eyes lock on the back windshield, trying to see if Hartley is upright or unconscious inside the vehicle. But before I can reach her, something heavy collides with my body and knocks me to the slick, icy asphalt.

It takes a half second for me to realize that Evgeny has run into me. He's flailing and screeching, trying to hit me with blood running down his face from a cut near his hairline. Blood drips onto my own face as I grapple with him for dominance. With a bellow of pure rage, I manage to grab him by the collar of his black duster jacket and flip us both over, pinning the bastard down. I pull back my arm and slam my fist down into his jaw with a cracking sound. He yowls in pain and jerks his elbow up into my cheekbone. I hear the thud of bone on bone and feel the deep ache, but nothing is broken. His aim is off, and I can tell the collision must have given him some kind of concussion.

"Get off of me, you fucking bastard!" he barks, still flailing at me with his fists, but every jab goes wide and misses completely.

"I'm not done with you yet," I hiss angrily.

I land another resounding punch to his bloody face. In the back of my mind, a small voice tells me I should stop, that Evgeny is a vital part of unraveling the plot he's set in motion. That he may be useless, but he has information that could exonerate Gerasim.

But a much louder voice tells me to kill him, to make him suffer for trying to steal Hartley away from me. I see crimson, my anger only intensifying with each strike.

He turns his head and spits out blood, then grunts through red-stained teeth, "What's the matter, Alexeyev? Don't want to share your toys?"

The rage inside of me goes nuclear. He can't talk about Hartley that way. My hand instinctively reaches for my gun, only to find that it's not there. It must have fallen out of my jacket during the collision. I immediately move on to the next best thing, roughly feeling Evgeny's body up for his own gun… but again, no gun.

He cackles, "At least it's a fair fight."

I plunge my hand down around his throat and squeeze, making him gag as his eyes bulge out of his head. I lean in close and hiss, "I don't need a gun to kill you."

I tighten my grip, watching the smugness change to

genuine fear as the life drains from Evgeny's face. I want to feel him die. I want to take his every breath for what he's tried to do.

And then, we're both drenched with snow kicked up by the squealing tires of his car. The driver must have come to. Despite the smoke billowing from under the hood and the tree branches impaling the windshield, the vehicle whips around. I look up just in time to see the driver essentially throw something out of the back seat, and it falls limply to the ground.

My blood runs cold when I realize it's Hartley's body. Suddenly, I don't give a damn about Evgeny anymore. I release him and dart to Hartley's side, giving the driver enough time to dart in and grab Evgeny. He tosses the rogue Avtoritet into the back seat and jumps into the front. The car goes flying off down the road with only one tail light left flickering, the windshield half-shattered, and deep dents along the front and right side. I don't know how far they will get, but right now, I don't care.

I cup Hartley's face in my hands, stroking her cold cheeks in an attempt to wake her up. She's dead weight in my arms, her eyes shut and her lips slightly parted. I lay my hand on her heart and feel it faintly thumping.

"Hartley. Hartley, wake up," I mutter, patting her cheek. Slowly, her eyes flutter open and she winces in pain, her hand reaching up to her jaw. I see that she has a bruise forming on the swell of her cheekbone. She draws in a few shuddering breaths and then bursts into tears. She flings her arms around me and sobs into my chest.

"I'm so sorry. I made a mistake. I-I got confused. I never, ever should have run from you, I see that now," she whimpers. I stroke her hair and gently rock her for a few moments.

"You don't have to apologize," I tell her. "I'm just glad you're alive."

"I'll *never* leave you again," she says fiercely, pulling back to look me in the eyes.

I lean down to kiss her softly. "I know you won't," I reply. "But we can't stay here."

I carefully get to my feet, pulling her up with me. She's wobbly, and I have a feeling her cheek bruise might not be her only injury, but she remains strong. Together we make our way back to my black sedan, which looks miraculously unscathed. But when I try to crank the engine, it won't turn.

"Shit," I swear to myself.

"Wait a second," Hartley says, holding onto the car to pull herself around to my side. I step out and watch with intrigue as she feels around the front left panel. Her face lights up when she fits her finger into a tiny hole, and presses a button. "Try it now," she says.

I turn the ignition and the engine sputters to life. With a grin, I help her into the passenger seat and ask, "What was that?"

She blushes as I slide behind the wheel again and the car starts rolling. "Inertia switch got flipped. It's a failsafe to protect the car after a collision like that," she replies. "All you have to do is press that little button to reset."

"And how did you know to check that?" I press.

Hartley looks wistfully out the window. "My dad refused to let me get my driver's license until I knew how to fix a car. At least, the easy fixes," she explains.

I shake my head in awe. "You continue to amaze me,

malyshka."

"Where are you taking me now?" she questions.

"The Pakhan—my superior—is hosting a lavish party tonight at his residence tonight. I have to get to him… and warn him," I explain.

"We're going to crash a party?" she asks incredulously.

"Essentially," I tell her.

The drive out to the Pakhan's house doesn't take long, with the streets so empty at night. The snow continues to fall, and it's a veritable winter wonderland when we arrive. The impressive mansion appears out of the darkness, separated from the neighbors by a massive amount of land, especially for New York. Even in the dark, we can make out the beautiful landscaping and architecture of the place. We park at the end of the long driveway, at the back of a line of cars. I cut the engine.

"Holy shit," Hartley breathes. She's gazing wide-eyed at the mansion. "Serious money."

"The man has a lot to lose," I agree cryptically. I reach under my seat to find my gun, which slid underneath it during the collision. I check it over to make sure it's not jammed or otherwise compromised, then tuck it into my jacket.

"Come on," I urge Hartley. We step out into the snowy air together.

I take her hand and she squeezes it. I can feel her nervousness as we stroll right up to the front entrance, but I keep my own pulse regular to help calm her down.

"Follow my example. Stay close. Act natural," I whisper to her as I knock at the door.

"Got it," she whispers back.

The door swings open and a familiar man is working

security. He's a Bratok of Arseny's, and he immediately gives me a nod to go on. I nod back, and lead my beautiful companion into the wild, ritzy world of underworld luxury. We step into the massive entry hall, with its sparkling chandeliers, mounted tapestries, elaborate furnishings, and grand double staircase. A live band plays upbeat jazz music while couples whirl on the dance floor. Men in black suits stand around the hall sipping vodka and chatting quietly. I look around and see mostly familiar faces. People acknowledge me, too, with a nod or simple greeting. But I'm on a mission. There's only one man I want to find: the Pakhan himself.

But he doesn't seem to be anywhere around. Starting to get more concerned, I enter the fray and ask a couple eager newcomers if they've seen him. Nobody can point me in the Pakhan's direction. Besides, the level of intoxication here is reaching dangerous levels. These are hard men with hard lives, and they play as hard as they work. This is supposed to be a rare opportunity to let one's hair down, so no one is on guard tonight. Nobody is worried about anything, much less the precise location of a man who thrives on secrecy.

I can't find him, but it only gets worse when I realize Hartley is no longer next to me. Somehow, she must have gotten separated from me as we pushed through the drunken crowd. I stare around in confusion. How did she slip away?

Was it intentional? She said she'd never run from me again. I trusted her. I could tell by her tone she meant what she said. So if she hasn't run away, that means *I've* lost her.

And with Evgeny and his driver still at large, I know it's vitally important that I find her.

CHAPTER 20

HARTLEY

In all my life, I have never seen such luxury in person. From the moment Zakhar's vehicle pulled to the end of the crowded, long driveway, my eyes have hardly closed for a second. I am surrounded by glamor, a tier of lifestyle I never could have even imagined. I may not have been on my own for very long, and I grew up pretty sheltered, but even I can recognize major money when I see it. Real estate is pricey in New York, even out on Long Island, away from the central hub in the depths of the city. Hell, even my tiny studio apartment in the Bronx cost an arm and a leg in rent. So this mansion, situated in a quiet, private lot off the beaten path, with all its fancy landscaping and decor, had to have come with a price tag that would nauseate a normal person. The 'Pakhan', as Zakhar keeps calling him, must be rolling in dough. The cars along the driveway were a bit less ostentatious, mostly mid-level sedans and coupes, with the occasional ritzy luxury brand mixed in. At the top of the driveway sits a three-car garage with the doors closed, but I can only imagine the high-dollar machines on the other side. They must also belong to the Pakhan, whose home only gets more opulent when we step inside.

The party is more like a gala, with a fancy live band and cater-waiters dressed in all black canvassing the grand hall, holding aloft trays of elegant hors d'oeuvres and champagne. There's also what looks to be a pair of bartenders mixing up custom cocktails at a mahogany-wood serving counter across the room. The music is lively and upbeat. People spin and whirl on the dancefloor, alone or in pairs, under the glittering giant chandelier. The hall is mostly cleared of furniture to make room for the long list of attendees, but what furnishings do remain are just as extravagant as the mansion itself. Everything looks like a well-kept heirloom piece, and each sofa or end table must cost thousands of dollars.

As Zakhar pulls me through the crowd, I'm over-whelmed by the sights, sounds, and smells of the grand hall. There's so much to look at, especially after being cooped up in that dull bedroom suite for a week. And after the night we've had, it feels nice to dip into a more cheerful atmosphere. The side of my face still aches from the impact of my cheekbone hitting the glass window in that horrible man's car. When I gingerly lift my hand to touch it, I wince at the pain. I know without even looking in a mirror that I have a bruise, but to my surprise, people aren't staring at me. Everyone is too busy having fun to notice Zakhar and I crashing the party.

Although… I suppose it's not 'crashing' a party if the doorman lets you in without a fight. Without a single word, actually. It makes me wonder more about Zakhar's reputation. Is this his usual crowd? Does he really hang out with a bunch of super-wealthy partygoers? It seems so distant from his personality, but maybe I just don't know him well enough yet.

As I walk through the ballroom, I realize that I don't know much of anything. I don't understand the intricacies of what's going on, just that I must be surrounded by connected, powerful people. Mostly men, I notice, except for the pretty dates on some of their arms.

I'm so caught up in observing the scene that it takes me a few minutes to realize I'm no longer with Zakhar. My heart pounds as I peer around in confusion. We were holding hands only minutes earlier! How could I have lost him? Fear seeps into my veins. I can't see very far, since the majority of the people here are several inches taller than me, and the crowd is dense. I manage to work my way to a wall and follow along until I reach one side of the grand staircase.

I start moving up the steps, hoping I'll have a better vantage point from higher up. But as I continue onward, I see no sign of Zakhar. He doesn't seem to be in the grand hall anymore, but I don't know where he went. So I keep going, and at the top of the staircase I come to a long, dark hallway. It's much quieter up here, the music and chatter muffled. I tiptoe down the hall, feeling for any open or unlocked doors. If nothing else, maybe I can find a bathroom to splash some water on my face and check out my bruise. At best, I might find Zakhar.

The hallway is decked out with old-looking portraits and tapestries, the wood floor covered in a long, intricate rug. There are gently smoldering sconces lighting my way along the walls. Most of the doors I come to are locked or empty, just sitting rooms or guest rooms with sparse but fine furnishings. A chill runs down my spine as I realize I'm probably not supposed to be up here. I can't get caught wandering around this rich, powerful man's house looking like a bruised-up mess. So when I hear what sounds like approaching footsteps and soft male voices, I panic and rush into the closest room. I shut the door in a hurry, and it's only when I turn around that my eyes go wide.

This is not a lifeless drawing room. It's not even a bathroom.

It's a surveillance room.

Why was it unlocked? My heart drops, and I wonder for a moment if it's a trap. I look back at the closed door behind me and I consider my options. I could head back out, pretend I got lost, and face who knows what. Or, I could stay in here and pray that someone had just gotten sloppy. Maybe the security guy ran to the washroom and was in too much of a hurry to lock the door?

Hell, even my parents would have made sure their security room automatically locked.

As I consider my options, I walk over to the wall of television monitors. There are ten in total, all displaying a different, crystal-clear angle of the mansion.

"Whoa," I murmur, taking a step closer.

Who requires this level of security? Who is this uptight about their property? I recall Zakhar's cryptic words about the Pakhan: *The man has a lot to lose.*

Suddenly, I hear what sounds like several people shouting all at once from downstairs. It's so loud that it startles me, and I rush to the door. But to my horror, the door seems to have locked from the outside somehow.

Oh sure, it autolocks from the outside, I sarcastically

grumble to myself. No matter how many times I try the knob, the door won't budge. I'm barred in, listening to the clamor happening outside. Maybe it was a trap. Or maybe someone saw me enter and wants me to watch what's about to go down.

Not like I have a lot of options.

I turn back to the monitors to watch the scene unfold.

In the grand hall, the live band has stopped playing. No one is dancing. They're running. Screaming. Shoving each other in their panic. I lean in close to see that some of the guests have guns drawn. I see the gunfire, the recoil, the bodies falling to the opulent floor. The gunshots are muffled and I realize the guns must be outfitted with silencers. The gunmen are making their bloody way up the stairs. My heart races as I scan the screens for Zakhar.

And it skips a beat when I finally see him, standing over another dead body as blood spills across the dancefloor. A second man approaches with his gun, but Zakhar doesn't shoot at him. In fact, they seem to know each other. He's moving through the crowd with his own gun raised and the other man close at his side, mirroring his movements. They work as a team, back-to-back as they clear a path to follow the original gunmen. I watch on the monitors as they go room to room, ready for a fight. They're cold-blooded professionals on the hunt, even as individuals break away to follow them. Zakhar and the other man are quick to neutralize each target, injuring them with a quick, non-fatal shot or even a quick jab of their fists.

I try the door again to no avail. I wish I could get out of here and reach Zakhar. I wish I had never gotten separated from him. I'm such a fool. Now I'm here alone and unarmed, and I can see Zakhar and his companion moving toward the other end of the same hallway I walked down to get here. I want to bang on the door, but I know it's a bad idea. It may not be Zakhar who answers.

But I have to move. I can't just stay locked in here. I refuse to let him down again.

I peer around the room, scanning it for escape options just like I did at the holding cell. Only this time, I find my exit: an air vent on the low ceiling.

"Am I really doing this?" I mutter.

Another shot goes off, and this one isn't silenced. I decide all at once I can't wait anymore. I have to be brave. So, in my knee-high boots and jeans, I clamber onto the desk below the monitors and stand on tiptoe. I manage to jump up and dislodge the vent cover. To my relief, there's no air coming through, and the vent looks just large enough for me to climb inside.

So I summon every fiber of my upper body strength to hoist myself up. It takes a few tries, but I finally pull myself up with my feet against the wall of monitors for support. The vent is tight and dark, with a slightly dank smell. I absolutely do not want to go forward, but I force myself to keep going. I take deep, slow breaths to combat my claustrophobia. I crawl along as quietly as I can, not knowing where in the house I'm located anymore. I simply follow the vent as far as I can in the same direction, until finally I hear voices again… much closer this time.

Coming from below. I cover my mouth to hide my breathing as I peer through the very narrow slats in the vent cover. I appear to be hovering in the ceiling of a gorgeously designed master bedroom, complete with a king-sized bed and a balcony. The voices get louder, and then the door to the bedroom bangs open. My breathing quickens as I watch several men pour into the room carrying weapons. It's not Zakhar and his companion, but I do recognize two of the men.

My heart sinks.

It's the man who tried to kidnap me just hours earlier, along with his chauffeur and a few big, burly men who are clearly his subordinates, as they lower their weapons after he does. All I can do is sit as still as possible and try not to let them hear me breathe.

CHAPTER 21

ZAKHAR

I keep my gun level as I climb the steps to the second floor. Arseny is right behind me with his barrel still pointing down the staircase. The two of us are an unstoppable pair, working in effortless tandem to clear a way through the mansion. Bodies lie strewn across the stairs in haphazard shapes. Their limbs twitch, their eyes bulging out of their heads. Some of them are just injured and calling out for help with raspy, desperate voices. Help doesn't come. There is nobody here to save them. Even when they reach out for me, clawing at my ankles, I simply step over them. Arseny and I are not strangers to death and suffering. Their blood dripping down the steps doesn't affect me.

At the bottom of the staircase, the grand hall is still a writhing mass of panicked partygoers. People scream and shout, running into each other, knocking themselves down in their haste to escape the carnage. The guest list seems to have been a veritable who's who of the Bratva. I recognized many of the faces I saw tonight, though most of the familiar ones disappeared when the violence broke out. It doesn't necessarily mean they're cowards—there were innocent people here tonight too. Even a mafioso has the chivalry to remove his civilian date from a dangerous situation and flee to safety. No doubt the roads back to Brooklyn are choked with getaway cars by now. The lesser-ranked among us don't have enough skin in the game to stay behind, especially since they probably weren't clued into either side of the violence tonight. In the fray, it's hard to tell friend from foe, and the two of us make a terrifying pair.

But we aren't done yet. In fact, we're just getting started. We have to find the Pakhan, and I have to find Hartley. Until then, there's not a force on earth that can slow me down.

We ascend to the top and lower our guns when we realize nobody is coming after us. The few remaining enemies who had tried to stop us now lay gurgling on the stairs. I hold up one finger to keep Arseny quiet as we look down the long, shadowy hallway. We stand still and listen. Above the downstairs din, I can hear the muffled tenor of male voices. I turn silently to Arseny and he nods, showing that he hears it too. We begin slowly, quietly making our way down the hall with our guns raised. We take turns trying each door as we pass while the other stands guard. After a few empty rooms, we both hear the jingle of keys, followed by a loud click.

A door just a couple feet away creaks open.

We both lift our guns and hold steady. Until a wizened hand reaches out the door and gestures for us to come closer. As soon as I see the wrinkles and various rings studding the man's hand, I know who it belongs to. I drop my gun and Arseny follows suit. We duck into the small room and Pakhan uses a large, vintage-looking set of keys to lock the door from the inside. Then he walks over to a broad computer interface of some kind and presses another button, and we hear the lock engage on the outside, too. Behind that interface is a wall of TV monitors, like a technologically fancier version of what I have at the safehouse.

"Thank god you're alright," Arseny says to the Pakhan. "It's madness out there."

"I know. I've been watching," the older man replies with a nod to the monitors.

"Did you catch who started this whole mess?" I ask.

The Pakhan smiles, but it doesn't touch his eyes. "I've only been in this room for a short time. But it would appear I'm not the only one to hide here tonight."

He points to the ceiling, and my heart sinks. The air vent cover has been shuffled aside, and I see light scuff marks on the desk. I have my suspicions, and sure enough, there's the faintest mark of a heel in the footprint.

"Hartley," I murmur, my stomach turning.

"Shit," Arseny sums up perfectly.

I step up to the monitors, scanning closely for any sign of her. Instead, I find only a group of men gathered in the Pakhan's luxurious bedroom suite. They're facing away from the camera right now, but I can see they're a hulking, black leather-clad bunch. And by the positioning and bulk under their arms, they have weapons.

"The hell are they planning?" I mutter.

"Your battle isn't over yet," the Pakhan says, resting his palm on my shoulder.

"I can get you to safety, sir," Arseny offers him.

I give him a grateful look. He knows I have to go on alone.

"We'll watch the monitors for a minute, make sure the coast is clear. Then I'll move us downstairs and out of the house," Arseny explains. "Does that sound okay?"

The Pakhan nods. "We'll take one of my untraceable vehicles. Scrubbed history and false license plate," he agrees, perfectly calm despite the near-massacre barely coming to an end just downstairs. At his age and position, he must have seen far worse than this.

"Good. Be careful," I urge them both.

"Same to you," Arseny says as the pair of them scrutinize the monitors.

As I'm turning to leave, a new sound erupts louder and more piercing than anything. A high-pitched, blood-curdling scream from down the hall. It sounds familiar because I've heard it before. It's Hartley, screaming for me just like she did hours ago when that traitorous bastard grabbed her off the street. My nerves steel into cold, hard, ruthless motivation at the sound of that scream. Twice in one night is too much. I never want to hear my beautiful little captive scream again—unless it's a cry of ecstasy at my hands.

"Oh fuck," Arseny swears. I look over his shoulder to see that Hartley is lying in the fetal position on the floor in the Pakhan's bedroom.

Surrounded by imposing men dressed in black. As they turn, I see Evgeny's face. He's gazing down at Hartley like the most precious gift has dropped into his lap. He's grinning.

Without another word or glance at the others, I bolt out of the surveillance room and down the hall. I can hear whimpers and raucous laughter as I dash to the bedroom door. As desperately as I want to go in guns a-blazing, I can't risk Hartley's life with my own recklessness. My life, sure. But never hers. So I press my ear to the flat wood and listen.

"Well, boys, you can't mess with fate. This little bitch managed to wiggle out of my grasp earlier tonight, but now look at us. Back together again," Evgeny cackles. "It's meant to be."

"Who is she, boss?" asks one of his Bratok.

He snivels, "One of Alexeyev's whores. Seems he's been holding out on us. Keeping her to himself like the selfish bastard he is. As if having the trust of the Pakhan isn't enough to lord over the rest of us."

"Please! Let me go," I hear Hartley whimper. My heart aches. My hands clench into fists. But I hold back, just for a moment longer.

"What do we do with her?" asks another of his men.

The dark, predatory laugh that comes from Evgeny's throat makes me see red.

"Whatever the hell we want. But as your Avtoritet, I call first dibs," he sneers.

I don't even bother with the doorknob. I knock the door in with one forceful kick, my gun raised at the backs of the men's heads. They whirl around at the loud bang, lifting their own weapons. In the first few seconds, I count two young men with knives, two men older than me with guns, Evgeny's favored Bratok and personal chauffeur who is unarmed but physically imposing, and of course, Evgeny himself holding the same small handgun he held to Hartley's temple on my mother's street earlier. He and the driver shrink back at the sight of me, the driver moving in front of Evgeny to protect him. The other four men drop in front of them to form a buffer between us. I immediately realize how dangerous gunfire could be in a room this densely packed. The suite is spacious for a bedroom, but not with seven bulky men and one helpless woman on the floor. A stray bullet could spell death in an area this tight.

"Zakhar!" Hartley wails.

One of the men fires his gun and the bullet goes whizzing inches from my head to lodge in the wall. It would be simple enough to fire back and eliminate him. But seeing Hartley on the floor reminds me why I shouldn't. Instead, I put away my gun and reach deep inside the interior pockets of my jacket to whip out two small, gleaming switchblades.

"Knives to a gunfight," Evgeny roars with laughter from his safe perch behind three layers of protective human shields.

His laughter is cut short when I suddenly tilt forward and charge right at the two younger men up front. I startle them, catching them off guard so they don't have a chance to properly prepare for the fight. They try to lift their knives in defense, but I plunge my blades into their forearms and rake downward. They each yowl with pain and drop their knives, clutching their wounded arms as blood spurts from their pumping veins. The one to my right dives at me and I dodge him easily, kicking out my leg to trip him. He tumbles to the floor and his knife goes clattering away just as the second knifeman comes at me with an angry yell. He tries to lift his arm to stab me, but his injured arm bends at the elbow and he drops the knife. I kick it back toward the door while tussling with him.

"Can't you give it a fucking rest?" Evgeny hurls from across the room. "I've had enough of your meddling and your stupid code of honor!"

"Shut your mouth, traitor," I hiss back through gritted teeth as I struggle with the attacker.

The gunmen behind him are trying to line up a shot at me, but I stay in constant motion, maneuvering the injured young man in front of me as we grapple. I punch him hard in the stomach and he buckles. He reaches up to try and push me away, his bloody hand slapping uselessly at my face. I twist his bleeding arm and he screeches in agony, dropping to the ground.

"Shoot him, you fools!" Evgeny barks.

Another shot fires off, this time going wide by a few feet to puncture an old-looking framed painting on the wall. I turn to the shooter with steam pouring out my ears. Any misfire could injure or kill Hartley. I have to stop these guys—for her sake if not mine.

The men are clearly taken aback by my unyielding rage. They're probably used to getting what they want with just the threat of their guns. But like I told Evgeny earlier tonight—I don't need a gun to kill him. I lunge at the shooter's legs, taking him down easily. The other gunman trips over Hartley on the floor and another wild shot goes off into the hardwood. Just a foot or so away from her. Enraged, I fling one of my small blades at his calf and it embeds in his flesh with a burst of crimson. He stumbles back on one leg, backing the driver and Evgeny against the French doors leading to the balcony.

"Get away from me! Kill him!" the evil Avtoritet shouts.

I've barely pinned the first shooter when the second

one points his gun at us. As he pulls the trigger, I roll the both of us so that he's on top of me, and I feel the man's body jerk violently when the bullet hits his spine. He goes limp and I shove him off of me, hopping to my feet as the shooter stares down in horror at his dying comrade. His disbelief gives me enough opportunity to yank the gun from his hands and put it in my jacket. Then I grab the now-unarmed man by the lapels and slam my head forward into his. I feel a dull, temporary ache, but the other man passes out almost in my arms.

Hartley yells, "Behind you!"

Still gripping the shooter, I whirl around just as one of the knife wielders comes dashing at me, blade raised. I fling his unconscious friend at him, knocking them both down. The first knifeman has given up on finding his weapon and is crawling toward the door. I grab the back of his jacket and hurl him out the door, slamming it shut. I hear the coward blubbering as he runs away down the stairs. I don't need to go after him; his fate has been sealed whether I'm the one who kills him or not.

As I'm turning back to the battle, the second knife wilder has clambered out from underneath his fallen companion. He goes running at me full-tilt and I brace for impact. But then, I hear Hartley cry out and my eyes dart over to see Evgeny's driver grab her by the throat and lift her off the ground. I hear the choked terror in her voice. I see the pain in her bulging eyes as she kicks uselessly. My distraction gives the remaining knifeman enough time to send his blade singing through the air. I feel a sharp tide of pain as his blade collides with my shoulder. He tries to pull back, but the knife is embedded too deeply in my muscle.

"No! Zakhar!" Hartley shrieks.

I come back to my senses long enough to rip the knife out myself with a spray of blood. My vision swims and my body sways from the attack, but I manage to pound the dull end of the knife into my attacker's chest hard enough to knock the wind from his lungs. With one hand pressed to my gushing shoulder wound, I use the other to beat the young Bratok down with the handle of his knife. He crumples to the floor and I step over his body before my own legs give out underneath me. I stumble down to my knees, clutching my shoulder.

"Drop the slut! I want her to watch him die," Evgeny snarls.

The driver kicks the knives away from me and throws Hartley down on the ground. Crying hysterically, she rushes to my side, trying to get at my wound as though there's anything she can do to help me.

She strokes my face and holds me, shaking as she watches the blood pump freely from the gaping wound. "No, no, no. This can't be happening," she mumbles tearfully.

I can feel the strength leaking from my muscles as the blood pours down my front. I stay still, my chin raised defiantly and my eyes glaring daggers at Evgeny. I hear the click of the French doors opening and see the driver backing into it, putting more distance between the evil pair and us. Since they clearly both think I'm finished, they take their time.

Evgeny steps in front of the driver and unfurls his own gun. As much as I want to embrace her for what might be the last seconds of my life, I push Hartley off of me, trying to get her out of the crosshairs. She goes stumbling away with tears streaming down her pretty face. She looks confused, her arms reaching out for me even as she sits crooked on the floor.

Evgeny gazes down at me smugly. He lets out a derisive snort.

"It's easy to be high and mighty as Obshchak, eh? But we'll see how arrogant you are with my bullet in your brain!" he threatens gleefully.

CHAPTER 22

HARTLEY

The whole scene unfolds in ugly slow motion. The fear I feel is so intense, I almost can't stand it. I'm half in my body and half floating around the ceiling, gazing down at the carnage in total disbelief that this is *my* life. The dead and injured lay about the floor like messy mannequins, staining the expensive flooring with crimson. The young man who stabbed Zakhar is gulping for his final breaths across the room, his arm flopping uselessly up at the doorknob.

As though there's any way to escape this hell. As though any of us have a chance.

Despite the blood and gore, despite the shadowy hauntings of my past, I've never seen a more horrific sight than my handsome, strong, dignified master on his knees. It isn't right. Rage and despair bubble up inside of me, watching Evgeny take a tiny, cowardly step forward to almost press the barrel of his handgun to Zakhar's forehead. I see his hands clench, his jaw tighten. Even with the blood pulsing down his front and his arm hanging at a disturbingly limp angle, he maintains his stoicism. He doesn't flinch. He doesn't blink.

He stares down death, daring it to take him.

Evgeny smirks like a horrible kid in a candy store.

"I've been waiting for this moment a long time, Alexeyev," he preens. "I would say 'don't take it personally, it's just business'. But it *is* personal now, Zakhar. I am going to deliver your corpse to the Pakhan myself."

"No," I mumble, tears still coursing down my face. But my sadness is shifting inside of me. The tears burn hot. My heart rate quickens.

"I look forward to my newfound freedom. Oh, the things I will do when you're not around to double-check everyone's ledger," Evgeny laughs. He glances at his chauffeur and adds, "We're going to be rich! As we should be."

"We should get moving, boss," the driver urges him.

"Don't tell me what to do!" Evgeny snaps. He pushes the gun harder into Zakhar's forehead, forcing him to lean back slightly.

Through it all, Zakhar remains silent. He doesn't look away. His strength is inspiring to me, and I feel that hot impulse within me growing brighter. The numbness that made me weak is dissipating as adrenaline leaks into my veins.

"But you're right. It's been too long, and I'm tired of wasting time," the bastard growls. "*Do svidaniya, Obshchak.*"

"Zakhar!" I wail.

Evgeny pulls the trigger and I brace for a spray of blood and brains, but it doesn't come. There's a loud bang, but instead of discharging a bullet, the handgun appears to recoil violently in Evgeny's grip and he drops it, stumbling back a couple feet in surprise. Time seems to slow down for me again, and all at once it all becomes clear.

The gun must have gotten jammed in the collision earlier tonight, and because Evgeny had an entourage of now-deceased men defending him, he hadn't tried to use the weapon since then. At the crucial moment, the damn thing turned on him. Zakhar doesn't have a bullet in his head, and both the driver and his evil superior are taken off-guard.

There have been few moments in my life that stand out as clearly as this one. All distractions melt away. My past is irrelevant, my future unpromised. But right now, in this precise moment, my instincts take over. The fear is gone, replaced with steely certainty that what I'm about to do is the right choice.

As Evgeny is stumbling back, clutching his smarting gun hand, I slip off one of my boots. On tingling legs I rise to my feet and close the space between us in a few short bounds. On the final leap, I lift the boot up over my head and back over my shoulder. Then, like splitting a log with an ax, I impale the thick, sharp heel of my boot deep inside the bastard's neck.

His screech of agony blends with the raw, animalistic cry ripping from my own throat. The driver reaches for me but I dart back out of his grasp, causing him to fall forward onto Evgeny, who's desperately pawing at the puncture wound as it spurts blood. They crash to the floor in a bloody, writhing heap. They're both slipping in the blood, panicking, trying to staunch the wound while they worm away from me on the floor. I'm still standing over them with the boot in my hand when Zakhar wobbles to his feet. I feel his heat, his presence. He puts a hand on my shoulder and I slowly lower the boot.

Evgeny is squealing like a pig, kicking and flailing as the distressed driver attempts to scoop him up. Zakhar starts striding toward them and the driver hoists up Evgeny, backing away onto the balcony. Even with his wounded shoulder, Zakhar walks tall and strong. He doesn't have a weapon, but the men are terrified. Evgeny is gasping and wailing. The driver is tripping over his own feet in his haste to get away.

But there's nowhere to go. Zakhar has them backed into a corner, with the railing pressed against the driver's back. I can hardly breathe, watching it all go down. Zakhar takes another aggressive step toward them and I see something change in the chauffeur's expression. He goes from pure terror to numb indifference as he realizes there's no way out. Still carrying Evgeny's body in both arms, the driver quickly turns and leaps from the balcony.

"Oh my god!" I gasp, clapping my hand over my mouth in horror. I rush to Zakhar's side, the winter air gusting around me as I gaze down at the broken heap on the lawn below. It's so dark outside, I can barely see the men, but I definitely don't detect any movement.

"Are they...?" I trail off.

"If we're lucky," Zakhar growls. "Come on."

He puts his good arm around me and leads me away from the balcony. He guides me through the carnage and down the hall to the staircase. I gawk at the bodies littering the grand hall. There's an eerie silence throughout the property that continues when we walk out onto the front lawn. The line of cars in the driveway have whittled down to a scattered few, some of which bear scuffs and dents from the inevitable panic that ensued here. People must have been running into each other trying to escape. I can hardly believe it—all this death, and yet somehow Zakhar and I are walking out alive.

The rush that comes over me at that realization is overwhelming. I feel an intense gratitude to be alive, and even more relief to have my incredible master still beside me. I'm in awe of him as we climb into his car and he turns the engine. The car pulls away from the mansion, leaving it and all its horrors behind.

"Are you hurt?" Zakhar asks, breaking the quiet.

"Me? I'm fine," I reply, turning in the seat to look at him. "What about you? Your shoulder… there's so much blood."

"Looks worse than it is," he answers. "But we're going straight to the doctor."

"A hospital?" I ask, wondering what kinds of crazy questions we'll get there.

"No. My doctor works all hours," he says.

It dawns on me we're not making a visit to a regular clinic—Zakhar has a doctor working for him. Maybe he works for the Pakhan, too. After everything I've seen tonight, I can't say I'm surprised. I'm just happy to know he'll get the medical attention he needs. My spirits lift higher with every mile we put between ourselves and that mansion. I start to relax a little, watching the snow flurry past the window as we roll down the dark back roads.

Not only did Zakhar prove beyond a doubt that he cares for me by risking his life to save me, but I've learned something about myself tonight, too. I've learned that I am stronger than I thought, and much braver when I have Zakhar at my side. He's devoted to me, and I am more than just a helpless victim; I am the companion he needs. I can keep up with him, and in a crucial moment, I can even save him. We rescued each other tonight, and the bond between us has strengthened to steel.

"I can't believe I did that," I mutter.

"You did well, Hartley. You were a very good girl," Zakhar tells me.

His voice is deep and velvety, and it makes my heart race. When he reaches over to lay his hand on my thigh, I feel like I might explode. How is it that I can be so turned on, not even an hour past the scariest confrontation of my life? I've been trying to outrun my past. I've been desperate to prove myself good, not evil. Not like my family. But I'm learning that good and evil are blurry concepts with a vast gray area in between. Maybe it's not for me to untangle. Maybe I'm just supposed to let love consume me.

Zakhar slides his hand slowly, centimeter by centimeter, up my thigh. I'm getting wet already, my body responding to his simplest of touches. I'm turning to face him, letting him squeeze my leg and drive me wild, when suddenly we're both blinded by a bright outpouring of light up ahead.

He pulls his hand back and we recoil from the light, blinking as our eyes adjust. The car slows down and skids a little on the icy roads. Finally, between beams of light, I start to make out the shape of several cars barricading the road up ahead, shining their brights at us.

Chapter 23

Zakhar

The headlights are so bright, it takes several seconds for me to even see the scene up ahead of us. The newcomers are obviously trying to blind us with their high beams. But my senses sharpen as I catch onto the situation. There are at least four large vehicles forming a blockade across the road. There are two SUVs and two trucks, all of which are shining their high beams directly at us. It's easy to figure out why. They want me disoriented so they can swoop in with the element of surprise.

My stomach lurches when I see movement. Men moving out from behind the cars, carrying guns and pointing them right in our direction. They pause in front of the vehicles, washed in eerie white light, and don't make any further motions toward us just yet. They are far enough away in the darkness for me to make out any specific features.

But as my eyes tick from one man to the next, I recognize their stance. Wide-legged, shoulders back, guns raised, heads slightly tilted to one side as their eyes peer through the crosshairs at us. Others stand unarmed between them, fists clenched at their sides. One of them carries a large blunt object, something like a club or a base- ball bat. They are dressed in all black, a couple even wearing balaclavas to better hide their identity. I reserve a special kind of contempt for those men in particular. Any man who wants to confront me had better have the respect to show me his face.

"Who are those guys?" Hartley asks, sinking down in the passenger seat.

"Can't see their faces yet," I reply in an undertone. "But they're definitely not allies."

She swallows hard. "What are they doing?" she mutters.

"Watching us," I answer shortly.

"Wh-why?" she presses.

I give her thigh one more gentle, reassuring squeeze before I reach inside my jacket and wrap my hand around my gun. I don't pull it out just yet, keeping my hand there, poised to whip and shoot if I have to.

My injured shoulder has stopped openly gushing blood by now. The dark burgundy splotches on my shirt are starting to dry. But there's no denying the fact that I'm at a disadvantage now, compared to my usual level of competence. I can still feel the faint pulse of blood up my arm. I have survived much worse injuries than this one, but it's no paper cut. My arm feels weak from lack of blood, and the hole in my muscle sends dull, throbbing pain through my arm, chest, and back. It's been difficult enough keeping that hand on the steering wheel as we drove away from the mansion. And now I have to face a whole team of enemies in the middle of a dark back road in the snow.

"Zakhar, they're coming closer," Hartley whimpers.

She's right. While a few of them hang back around the headlights holding their guns, a group of three others come rushing forward. I lock the car doors and get my gun ready. We're outnumbered. Outmanned. Outpowered. All we can do is get the hell out of dodge.

"Hold on," I command Hartley.

I throw the car into reverse and slam my foot down on the gas. The engine roars as the tires kick up a rain of churned ice. We start skidding backward and I'm about to back us out of here when several loud cracks split the air: gunfire.

Immediately, the car goes wildly swerving in a circle as three out of four tires split open. The car lurches to one side and comes to a dragging, gravelly stop. The smell of burnt rubber fills the snowy air as we finally come to a stop.

The fuckers shot out my tires.

Hartley is hyperventilating and sobbing in the car beside me. I barely have time to turn to her and look her over for injuries before the men start dashing toward us. They're shouting and whooping like hunters trailing a shot bird. I kick open my car door and jump out, holding up my gun as the men swoop toward Hartley's side.

"No! Get back!" I snarl, firing several bullets in that direction.

The men aren't fazed in the least. None of them are hit, and they keep coming. I tuck my injured arm and make a leap onto the top of the car, roll across, and slam the blunt end of my gun into one of the attackers' heads. He howls in pain and stumbles backward, clutching his head. Meanwhile, the other two are trying to rip open the locked passenger side door, while Hartley screams on the other side of the window.

Her scream strikes deep inside me, that animalistic, instinctual place. For a few moments, I feel no pain. I use my injured arm to shove back one of the men while I knee the other one in the gut. The first guy comes running back to tackle me, and even though he's smaller than I am, my hurt shoulder betrays me. He's able to pin me down, pull his fist back, and land one square punch to my jaw. I fight for grip of my gun with my good arm, but I don't get an opportunity between blocking his hits. From the ground, I hear the men cheering cruelly, Hartley wailing my name in utter terror, and the revving of engines. I'm fighting for my life, fighting for her life, too.

But it's not enough. Because then, I hear gunshots even closer, and shattered glass sprays out over the both of us. The next thing I know, the men are dragging Hartley out of my car. I summon my strength to headbutt the man atop me, kick him in the crotch, and roll away from him. As I'm getting to my feet, my vision swims. I'm getting disoriented and increasingly dizzy from blood loss and exertion. My legs feel like lead as I chase them down. I pull out my gun and point it at the kidnappers, but they're smart enough to carry Hartley like a human shield, and there's no shot I can safely make.

"Please! Don't let them take me!" she sobs, kicking and screaming like a feral cat.

But they're already bundling her into the back of an SUV while a barricade of men blocks me from her. I stand dripping blood and completely aghast in the street. All but one of the men pile into the various vehicles and drive off at top speed, leaving icy rivets in their wake. I watch the cars disappear in disbelief. Sorrow strikes like another knife to the flesh, but it's quickly replaced with a more productive, useful energy: rage.

The one man remaining is the one with a baseball bat. He's a young guy, scrawny and nervous with big eyes. He's the last one guarding me, in front of his pickup truck. His clothes and vehicle are less impressive than the others. I can tell he's green, and that's why they've left him behind with me. Seniority gets the best job. New guys get the slop work, the dangerous stuff. This poor guy can't be older than nineteen, and they've left him with the short straw: the job of holding me back.

In other words, his superiors have left him here for slaughter. A casualty of war. Another pawn to sacrifice for the protection of the back line. They know I'm likely to kill him, and they don't care. The guy probably knows that, too, judging by his hands shaking as he holds the bat.

I slowly walk up to him, an idea in mind.

"St-stay back!" he shouts, but he sounds terrified.

I ignore his command and continue approaching. He brandishes the bat, but I pull out my gun and point it right at him. In a voice colder than the ice on the road, I glare at him and instruct, "You will step away from the truck and throw me the keys."

"What? No, I'm sorry. I can't let you do that!" he shouts back.

I cock the gun, showing him I'm serious.

"Your friends left you here to die," I remind him bluntly. "They want me to kill you."

The young guy falls silent. He knows I'm right.

"If you don't do exactly as I say, I *will* kill you," I go on. "Now, step aside, and toss me the fucking keys."

After a moment's hesitation, the guy lowers his bat and shuffles to the side of the road. He looks totally despondent as he takes out the keys and throws them to me. I catch them easily in my good hand, give him one nod of respect, and slide into the truck. I jam the keys into the ignition, the engine sputters a little and turns on. The whole truck rattles, and I can tell it's not in fantastic shape. Still, it's probably that man's pride and joy. It's torture for him to watch me drive off in his vehicle, but at least I left him with his life. As for my black sedan, that's a problem for the future. Right now, I have to catch those bastards who took Hartley.

I push the decades-old truck as hard as it can go. I whirl around the icy curves, plowing through the darkness with my headlights off. I don't want them to see me coming. There are moments when I can hear the convoy of cars thrumming somewhere down the road. I speed up to catch them and somehow lose them again in the darkness. There are only a few different ways to go out here, and I'm determined to stay on the right trail. But it's quickly becoming apparent that this is an unfair battle. Between the truck struggling to keep up and my shoulder injury rendering my arm more and more useless, I'm falling too far behind. I'm getting desperate.

With my eyes still on the road ahead, I take out my phone and dial Arseny's number. It rings twice and he picks up, to my relief.

"Zakhar, are you okay?" he asks.

"No. They took Hartley," I tell him. "I'm tailing them

now, but this damn truck can't keep up. I have some ideas about where they're heading, but I need backup."

"I've taken the Pakhan to the headquarters about twenty minutes from the mansion. I'm not far from you now. Where to, boss?" he asks.

"Try the safehouses. And the warehouse," I add. "I'll update you."

"Great. I'll meet you where the battle starts," he answers dutifully, and hangs up.

I dig my foot into the gas pedal even harder. My mind whirls in a hundred directions. Who is behind all of this? Could it be Evgeny's men? I've already taken out his Bratoks, and we left the bastard himself broken and mangled on the mansion lawn below that balcony. So, if not him, who else? Who could Hartley be running from? I wonder again about her family, about where she comes from. Who was she so afraid of that she had to change her name? And why pick the name she chose? Why New York City?

There are so many questions I've yet to answer about her. So much left to explore. And I'll be damned if I let anyone—I don't care who—take her away from me before I get a chance to find out.

CHAPTER 24

HARTLEY

Fear drips through my veins like ice water. My body is so exhausted by this point. I ache all over as I lie bound and blinded in the dark trunk. I don't know what time it is, but it must be getting late into the night. Maybe even early morning. I have been awake and active since the last morning, which seems like a lifetime ago by now. The version of me who strolled into that police station to steal evidence is gone. I thought I was scared then, sneaking around the evidence lockers, getting caught by a secretary. But my little crime moment pales in comparison to the stress of this night.

So many hands touching me, leaving ugly fingertip bruises all over my skin. So many horrible faces, twisted in cruel laughter as they loom over me. I resent the version of myself who feared Zakhar. I thought I knew true danger. I thought I could handle myself. But if not for my handsome, mysterious master, I would be surely be dead… or worse, tortured in the grasp of fat less virtuous men.

If I had any doubts about Zakhar's intentions with me before, tonight has eliminated them.

It turns out, enemies are around every corner. Who knows how many times I blissfully floated through a near-death experience while I was living as Maggie in the Bronx? I thought I could disappear into the city, get lost in the thick swarms of people, but I was naïve.

It was so easy for Evgeny to grab me, and now someone else has done the same. I feel so defeated. Tears roll down my cheeks silently, dampening the rough carpet under my cheek. My arms are bound behind my back, my ankles tied together with my knees drawn up to my chest. I'm curled up in the trunk, being jostled and slung around the corners. I can feel the rumble of asphalt under the tires and the slick spray of ice as the SUV thunders along. Every time there's a bump or slippery patch, my stomach churns. Nausea builds up in my chest. My hands are going numb as I shiver in the bitter cold of the unheated trunk.

It takes some time for my ears to adjust to the combination of white noise and begin to separate the human voices from inside the SUV. Up front, I hear two voices, one gruff and one a little higher pitched but still undeniably male.

"Where to, boss?" asks the higher voice.

"The old pawn shop. Remember? We've been over this," answers the gruff voice.

"Do you think Fyodor can handle the Obshchak on his own? It's his first mission. He doesn't even have a firearm yet," asks the first one.

"Sink or swim. Fyodor is a pussy," is the dismissive reply. He chortles, "Maybe a little danger will put some hair on his chest."

"He's just a kid."

"Exactly. So we're not losing one of our best soldiers. There's a reason for everything."

There are a few moments of quiet.

"How long do we have to hold onto the pretty one?" pipes up the higher voice.

"Let me get Whitlow on the phone," sighs the gruff one.

My heart drops into my stomach.

It can't be.

I hear the sound of a line ringing over speakerphone. Time slows down as it rings three times, each one seeming to last forever before finally someone picks up.

"Do you have her?" growls the familiar voice on the phone.

The hairs on the back of my neck stand up. My heart skips, almost painfully. The nausea in my gut rises, and I gag, almost throwing up.

That voice haunted my adolescence. It still plays in my head, saying the most horrible accusations, even to this day. I escaped him, but I could never escape my memories, except for in those blissful moments with Zakhar.

"Yes, sir. The girl is in our custody and we will arrive shortly," answers the gruff voice, with an added punch of formality like he's addressing a superior.

"What about the guard dog?" asks my father.

"We shot out his tires and left a man behind to restrain him," the kidnapper responds. "He's not going to be a problem, I swear."

"We will eliminate him in good time. The structures are shuffling. He can't close in on us like he wants to. Who will answer to him? Who will remain loyal to a man who has lost everything?" my father boasts.

"No one, boss," grovels the gruff man.

"What is a man without his greatest possessions?" my dad goes on. He laughs cruelly, "If I didn't despise him so much, I might thank Alexeyev for capturing my little runaway. Unfortunately, I have a feeling he didn't keep her in mint condition. I assume I will receive a damaged version of my daughter tonight. It's too much to expect a whore like her to keep her legs closed. She takes after her mother. Stupid. Weak. But I've made some improvements to my bunker. She won't be able to escape me ever again."

The tears sting in my eyes. I grit my teeth, wishing I could swipe the tears away. I don't want him to be right—I don't want to be weak. All those old feelings come washing back over me. I've tried to crush my memories of growing up in that fortress of a house, under the conniving claws of my father.

I remember standing at my barred window, watching the world go on without me. Days so long and dark and empty they felt like nights. So many whispered conversations just around the corner or behind a locked door. So many secrets. No one told me anything.

My mother was just a wisp of a woman, barely present enough to look after herself, much less my brother and I. She was always drifting through the house in a dressing gown, pills in her pockets and a distant look in her eyes. She was a captive too, and so cowed by years of mistreatment that she could no longer stand up for herself. Or for us.

Tommy, my brother, was a rowdy, playful kid. As very young children, we were close. Our world was so tiny, how could we not be? But over the years, our paths split.

The differences between our upbringing became more glaringly apparent.

He and Dad butted heads sometimes, but even when we were still kids, I saw the contrast between how he treated Tommy and me. My brother was allowed to play outside, have friends, even play sports sometimes despite our homeschooling. I stayed cooped up in my second story bedroom while Tommy rode off into the night with a car full of friends. He came home less and less. We spoke rarely, then not at all.

That left me with only one soul to look after and love me: the one non-family member living in our enforced house upstate. Her name was Maggie, and she was hired to clean and cook for our family when Dad realized how little interest Mom had in doing so.

Maggie was kind and gentle, attentive in a way no one had been with me before. She took her time to show me how to cook each recipe, guiding my hands even when I was too young to be actually helpful. She made my favorite macaroni and cheese when I was sad, and home-made chicken soup when I was sick. She snuck extra cookies to my room when Dad had one of his paranoia flare ups and locked me in. She made me smile and laugh with her silly antics or nonsensical jokes. She brought a light to our dark fortress, a glimpse of how normal people lived. I knew that she was my dad's employee, so I never felt entirely safe with her, but she was the closest thing I had to a friend. A parent.

That is, until Dad decided that Maggie was part of the problem. He hated how close we were. He hated knowing that Maggie had earned my love in a way he never would. His sick mind twisted against her, and before I even had a chance to say goodbye, Maggie was gone. I never saw her again. And I never felt that warmth she gave me again… until I met Zakhar.

Now, I know what it feels like to be loved.

"Hartley will finally be mine. Home where she belongs. Where I can make sure nobody ever touches my little girl again," my father concludes and rage boils up in me. My nails dig into the flesh of my palms, and all the hate and hurt that he'd seeded in me over my first twenty-one years bursts to life.

"Are you going to punish her, boss?" the gruff man beseeches eagerly.

My father chuckles grimly. "I wouldn't be a good father if I let her sins go unpunished. Trust me, she will rue the day she left home."

ZAKHAR

The old truck's headlights flicker weakly as it flies down the icy back road. Snow falls heavily, blanketing the world around me and reducing visibility to nearly nothing. The truck has clearly been through a lot, and it's quite a step down from my usual luxury sedan, which is specially outfitted for speed, precision, and storage. But my own car is miles and miles behind me now, sitting crooked on the side of the road with all four tires shot flat. I have a fleeting wonder about the young man I left behind at the scene. I don't feel guilty—he's working with my enemy, and that makes him no friend of mine—but I don't wish death upon the kid either. He's too green to have much of a say in his life, especially if he's entangled with the mafia. He doesn't deserve to freeze to death in the middle of nowhere in a snowstorm.

But right now, that guy is the least of my concerns. All I can think about is getting Hartley back in my arms again. And with my wound still bleeding, and the dark, snow, and weak truck engine slowing me down, it's not going to be an easy mission. I can't catch up to the convoy of vehicles that took her, but I have a secret tool.

Using my good arm to steer the car, I use my weaker one to pick up my phone. I slide open a tracking app and watch as the map triangulates down to a specific location. The little green pin flashes on the screen, the distance between here and there counting down by the mile.

It's a tracking device embedded in the collar I gifted to Hartley. The collar looks so dainty and unobtrusive, no one would suspect there's a deeper use to it.

She hadn't taken it off since, even without my having to tell her, thankfully. It wasn't that I didn't trust her to know about the tracker, it's just that sometimes, being kept in the dark is for her own safety.

Unless they've totally stripped her down—and for their sakes as well as hers, I hope not—she will still be wearing it. Meaning that wherever that green pin flashes, that's where I'll find Hartley.

They've stopped moving. They've reached their destination. The GPS map zooms in as I get closer, and I recognize the location as an old pawn shop, mafia-run but civilian-fronted, out toward Northville. As soon as I'm certain, I drop the location to Arseny's phone so he can follow me out there… in case backup is required.

I focus hard as the truck rolls closer to the pawn shop. The engine makes a clunky chugging sound, so I decide to ditch the truck about a quarter mile from the pawn shop. I pull over on the shoulder and step out into the frigid darkness. My good arm keeps my gun close as I sneak around the back of the pawn shop. There are several vehicles here which I recognize from earlier. The front part of the building is dark, but there's a light shining in the back room.

This is definitely the spot.

I creep along the brick wall to the partly-open back door with my gun ready. I take a few moments to make sure no one is manning the back entrance before I silently slip inside. It smells dank and moldy here. The back of the shop is relatively large, with rows and rows of metal shelving. Some of the shelves contain the usual pawn shop items—watches, jewelry, knickknacks. But others are stacked with what looks like tinned food, emergency kits, and other items you might use in a crisis. It looks like the hoard of a doomsday prepper.

And through the shelving I can see a scene unfolding under the dim light of a single bulb hanging overhead. Fury lashes up in my body when I see two men drag a weeping, exhausted Hartley across the room to drop her in front of a tallish, middle-aged man in a suit. Her ankles and arms are bound, and she's on her knees, looking up at the man with pure hatred. The man is so imposing, it takes a minute for me to clock the silvery-haired woman standing several steps behind him. She is beautiful in a familiar sort of way, but there's no life to her. She watches the scene unfold without a flicker of emotion or even recognition. I wonder what the woman must have gone through to end up this way.

The man bends down in front of Hartley and says, in a condescending tone, "Tell me, daughter of mine, have you enjoyed your little adventure in the big, wide world?"

It all clicks into place. This horrible man is Hartley's father. The beautiful, empty woman is her mother. And

this is the fate Hartley was running from when I
found her.

Hartley crumples in front of her father. Already on her
knees, she somehow shrinks even smaller as the tears drip
down her face. The cruel man caresses her soft blonde hair,
but not with love—with the detached interest of a man
surveying a prized racehorse. She tries to pull away, but he
grabs her chin and holds her there. Rage bubbles in my
chest again.

"Silly girl. You can't escape me. You're part of this
family, whether you like it or not. You've wasted a lot of
precious time and manpower with this little stunt. But it's
no matter. Soon, you will be safe at home with me, where
you belong. I have given you too much slack. It's time to
tighten the leash. You're never leaving me again," he
sneers.

Hartley is still crying, but I see something change in
her expression. She sniffs, "When I was a little girl, I
thought you were protecting me from evil. I thought you
kept me locked away for my own good."

Her father smiles and strokes her cheek. "It's true. I do
it for you, princess."

"But I was wrong," she continues defiantly through her
tears. "You never cared about me. You never wanted to
keep me safe. You only wanted to keep me in a cage for
your own enjoyment. It's the same reason you hoard all
these supplies. So you could look around at all the things
you own and feel proud of yourself. Better than everyone
else. I'm nothing to you—just another item to gather dust
while you live your life in the real world. Well, fuck that!"

Her father's face is going purple with rage. "How dare
you speak me to me that—"

"No! I won't let you control me anymore!" Hartley interrupts passionately. "You can take everything from me. You can keep me in a tower. But I will never believe a word you say. I will never give you an inch of satisfaction. And I will never, *ever* be your little girl again."

Her father huffs angrily and pulls his arm back to hit her.

He doesn't get the chance.

Before his fist can connect with Hartley's perfect face, I send a bullet whizzing through the air. It flies just past her father's face and rips through the chest of one of his henchmen. I manage to fire off several more shots in the dark and the men drop like flies, all wounded enough to stay down. They're desperately trying to staunch their wounds and fumble for their weapons at the same time, but I have the advantage.

I stick to the shadows, darting behind one shelf to the next, avoiding the few shots the others get at me. Hartley's parents are both on the floor by now, ducked down with their arms over their heads in terror. Holding out my gun, I rush out into the open. Two more henchmen come hurtling at me as Hartley's father barks commands on the ground. I parry them with my good arm, fueled by pure adrenaline.

"Zakhar!" Hartley cries out.

The relief and adoration in her voice fills me with even more brute force. I scoop her up and she leans into my chest, my wounded arm draping around her as I hold my gun to her father's forehead. The old man looks up at me in confused horror.

"Wh-who the hell are you?" he demands to know.

"I am the man who made your little girl a woman," I

fire at him, knowing how much the words will scald him. "And I'm the man who will keep her safe. From you."

I ready the trigger and Hartley lays a hand on my chest to stop me.

"No. Don't kill him," she says softly.

Her voice stays my hand, but I tell her father, "Your daughter offers mercy. I'm sure she never learned that from you. And if you ever come after her again, I guarantee not even she can stop me from putting a bullet in your brain."

As we're backing away together, Hartley delivers one final line to her parents.

"Now you know how it feels to be betrayed by your own family," she says icily.

With that, we back out of the building into the snowy night. I hastily untie her ankles so we can run. Our footsteps crunch through the snow, adrenaline pumping as we leave the pawn shop—and Hartley's haunting past— behind us. As soon as we reach the old truck, Hartley turns to me with shining eyes, her beautiful face rosy in the cold.

I can't resist another moment. All night, I've been desperate to hold onto this girl, and now, finally, she is truly mine. I hold her face in both hands and gaze into her eyes. I lean in and press my lips to hers. She moans and melts against me, pinned between my body and the side of the truck. The truest love I've ever felt radiates between us. The cold, the wound, the exhaustion—none of it matters. She soothes my pain and warms my soul, melting the snow around us as we deepen the kiss. I need her all to myself, and I need her now.

Chapter 26

Hartley

Snowflakes swirl gently through the dark. They land delicately on my hair and lashes as I sink into the arms of my master. My savior. My whole entire world. His lips are simultaneously soft and hard against mine, his tongue gently pressing into my mouth. I love the feeling of his hard, heavy body leaning into me, and I hardly notice the slick, frigid metal of the truck behind me. The cold sits back a few feet, like it just can't penetrate the glow of warmth between us. Zakhar's large, capable hands cup my face while his cock stiffens against my hip. I can't help but roll forward on my heels to rock into him, showing him without a single word just how much I want him. How much I *need* him.

After what we've just been through together tonight, there is no question left in my mind as to whether we're meant to be. The whole universe has tried to pick us apart. Enemy after enemy appear to separate our souls, but they can't deny fate. None of us can. Besides, Zakhar has proven again and again that he would do anything to keep me, even if destiny itself had other intentions. He has made his claiming mark on me, and I know who I belong to.

Zakhar breaks our kiss to gaze into my eyes, his forehead resting against mine. He strokes my face and hair for a few moments, like he's making absolutely sure I'm real.

"How did you know where I was?"

His rough fingers graze against my cheek, his eyes penetrating mine.

"I will always know where you are. As long as you are mine," he says, holding my gaze. His words sink in, and he doesn't need to say anymore. I understand, instinctively, that as long as I keep his collar, he can find me, and it fills me with a warm comfort.

"Where do we go from here?" I ask quietly.

"Someplace safe," he answers. "Come along."

He helps me into the old truck, slides behind the wheel, and we're off. The truck isn't as smooth a ride as his luxury sedan, but we don't care. I'm elated to be not only alive but free, and not only free but running off toward sunrise with the man I love. We barrel away down the road, leaving my tangled, ugly past behind us. Hopefully, my family has gotten the message this time. I'm gone, and I'm not coming back. I'm not a part of that family anymore—hell, I never really was. I have a real family now in Zakhar, and he will protect me at all costs.

The tension between us grows with every mile we drive. In the tight cab of the old truck, the air is steaming up. Zakhar steals a sultry sidelong glance. I scoot a little closer across the bench seat so that my thigh is touching his. My hand rests with one finger on his leg for a moment, waiting for the right cue. His cock twinges with need and I slide my hand over, sucking in a tight breath of longing when I feel his stiffness. I lick my lips and begin to stroke up and down the thick shaft of his cock, straining through his pants. At the same time, I slip my other hand up the bottom of my sweater. I moan as my hand gropes and caresses my tits. I roll my nipples between my thumb and forefinger while I massage the growing bulge at Zakhar's crotch.

I'm getting slick between my own legs, my clit starting to ache. Zakhar's hands are gripping white on the wheel, his jaw tensing as he keeps his eyes on the road. My fingers itch with the desire to unzip his pants, finally touch his hot skin and straining cock. Luckily, I don't have to wait too long.

The safehouse emerges from the frosty fog. It's a beige-brick bungalow with a derelict, wire-fenced yard. Snow piles over the long, dead grass. There are no lights —not even on the street. It looks like no one has occupied the building in decades. But when we crunch through the deep snow to the front door, I see there's a tiny keycode box affixed to the icy lock. I shiver and look around in the darkness while Zakhar types in a surprisingly long code. There's a mechanical clicking sound and the door gently tilts open, like it's been waiting for us. Despite the abandoned appearance, a gust of heated air rolls over us. A dim light flickers on to reveal a charming but no-frills interior outfitted with cottage-y furnishings. Zakhar shuts the door behind us, and the howling winter winds fall silent. The locks engage automatically, and we're safe.

"Finally," I sigh.

"Finally, and forever," Zakhar growls, crossing the

room to scoop me into his arms for another passionate kiss.

His hands slide around me, smoothing down my back to squeeze my ass. I rock into him, moaning when I feel his cock hard against me. We grind against one another as we kiss, the desperation growing sharper every second. Even though we've escaped several layers of immediate danger tonight, the adrenaline is still pumping. The chemicals of stress, excitement, fear, and desire collide together in a burst of raw impulse. I forget every insecurity. I step away from my own ego and give myself over completely to my master's bidding.

Zakhar peels my sweater up over my head and tosses it aside. He sweeps me back into his good arm and I lean back, letting his lips trail down my jaw to my ticklish, bare neck.

He kisses down my throat and up to my ear, nibbling at my earlobe before whispering, "If not for this collar, I might've lost you."

He slips one finger under the collar, pulling it tight around my neck. The constriction gives me a thrill instead of fear, and I feel my clit twinge with need. His deep voice rumbles, "Perhaps now you understand everything I have done to protect you, how far I will go to keep you mine."

"I do," I whisper back.

"Good girl. Get on your knees for me, *malyshka,*" he instructs.

I obey. I immediately kneel before him, topless and guileless, awaiting command. I gaze up at him in wide-eyed awe. I love how he makes me feel so small, how he shows me his strength without showing off. Even with his injured arm, he's the one in command.

His good hand pats my cheek, then he slowly unzips his jeans. My mouth waters as I watch the zipper descend and the black fabric of his boxers come visible. Without removing his pants or boxers, he takes out his massive, glorious cock. I splay out my tongue and he rewards me by wrapping my long hair around his hand, holding me tight in his fist. He keeps me in place while he pushes his cock against my lips. I allow him inside eagerly, slurping my tongue around his engorged tip. My pussy clenches when I taste precome on my tongue, but I have to stay still.

Zakhar is totally in control, rocking his hips to slide his cock in and out of my mouth while he grips my hair. His velvety heat slides up and down my tongue, poking deeper and deeper into the back of my throat so that I almost gag. Saliva drips down my chin and onto my breasts as Zakhar pumps into my warm, wet mouth. I groan with pleasure when he picks up speed, pummeling into my throat with his enormous shaft until tears burn in my eyes. He tugs at my hair, moving me up and down on his cock while I splutter for air. I feel him going extra stiff on my tongue, his muscles tensing for climax. But he's not finished with me yet. Before I can happily suck the life out of his cock, he pushes me back. He slips out of my mouth with a wet smacking sound. My cheeks ache, my throat all scratchy, but I want more.

Zakhar pulls me to my feet and wraps his good arm around me, walking me back to pin me against the wall. He quickly unzips my jeans and pushes them down. I kick them off and groan when he pushes his leg between my thighs and ruts against me, causing delicious friction underneath my panties. He grabs my wrists and holds them over my head with one hand, then slides it back down the front of my body. I keep my hands above my head dutifully, even as his searing touch elicits ticklish gasps from my throat. He gropes my chest lewdly, tweaking my nipples on his way down my flat stomach to my aching mound. He leans close to graze my neck with his teeth while his fingers begin to stroke my labia, with only the thin panties between us. Zakhar massages me through the delicate fabric until it soaks through with my juices. Then, he slips my panties aside and gives my clit a soft, stimulating pinch.

I shiver with pleasure and feel my knees buckle beneath me. But Zakhar holds me steady, even as his fingers work me into a tizzy. My breaths come ragged and quick while he strokes my slick flower, delving between my petals before sliding back up to my throbbing clit. I pant and moan in his grasp, tossing my head side to side as that tight-wound bead of tension intensifies. Every muscle in my body clenches around his touch. My mind goes blank, save for the relentless, buzzing pleasure ratcheting ever higher. Zakhar is staring into my eyes now, commanding me not to even blink while he unravels me with one powerful hand. I can barely remember to breathe, the need for release is so strong.

My master holds back the tide of pleasure with a command, "Not until I say so."

CHAPTER 27

ZAKHAR

I have Hartley trembling in the palm of my hand. Her chest heaves with each laborious breath, her breasts jiggling deliciously. Her hair is a tousled mess and her cheeks are flushed rosy pink. The BDSM collar sits pretty on her throat, and it moves faintly when she swallows hard. I hold her clit between two fingers while my thumb drags a tantalizing line up and down. I dip between her slick folds and sweep back up to massage that tight bundle of nerves. Each pass makes her whimper and moan, and I feel her honey drip down my fingers. My precious girl is on the edge of coming, but she's at the mercy of my will. Her body won't let her come until I give permission. Seeing how obedient she is makes my cock stir. She's desperate for release, and every time I deny her, the need grows more intense. Her lips shine with saliva. Her eyes shimmer with held-back tears. She's shaking like a flower drenched with morning dew, perfect and vulnerable, waiting for my touch alone to make her bloom.

I pinch her clit tighter than before and utter the simple command, "Now."

"Ohhh," Hartley mewls.

Her body melts into violent tremors as my fingertips rub her clit in hot, tight circles. My beautiful girl tips her head back and moans as her pussy gushes come all over my hand. Her juices slick down her thighs, making a sticky mess. It's not enough to feel it—I want to taste her, too. She's still trembling when I kneel down and hook her leg over my good shoulder. I push her back into the wall, shoving her thighs apart so I can dive in. I nuzzle into her glossy cunt, inhaling her specific, delightful fragrance. I collect her honey on the tip of my tongue before devouring her with abandon. I flick my tongue over her folds and dip down to tease the band of nerves around her opening. I slide back up, making my tongue rigid as I swirl around her clit. I focus on the knot of nerve endings, tonguing her clit until I feel her clench up and release again.

"Mmmm, yes," she sighs as her juices flood my tongue.

I rock back on my heels and grab her waist, spinning her around so that her cheek is pressed to the wall. I grope her juicy, lush ass cheeks, reveling in how soft her flesh is under my touch. I spread her legs wide apart, admiring her pussy and tight little asshole. I run my tongue down the sensitive crack and around to her clit. I grab and smack her ass, making it jiggle as I eat her cunt from behind. Her ample breasts push into the wall and she nudges back into me, rocking her pussy back and forth against my lips. I flick my tongue between her pussy and ass, making my gorgeous girl squirm with pleasure. It doesn't take long for her to come again, her body shaking and covered in goosebumps as she gushes on my tongue.

This time, I stand up and press into her from behind. I lean over her shoulder and she turns her head to meet my lips. I kiss her deeply, letting her taste herself while I smack my hard cock against her ass. I nibble the side of her neck and position my length at her quivering hole. I rub the engorged head around the opening, slicking it up with her own juices. Hartley pushes back into me, and I know she's silently begging me to fuck her.

"Mine. All mine," I grunt in her ear.

She nods eagerly, rutting back against me so that my cock nearly presses inside of her.

"Please… I'm all yours," she breathes. "Take me, Master."

I don't need another invitation.

Pinning her against the wall with her wrists above her head, I grab her hips and hold her in place while I shove into her. Hartley's legs shake and go weak as I enter her, but she regains her strength and braces herself against the wall while I slide inside her in one swift, forceful motion. Hartley whimpers, her fingertips curling in as her lips fall open in an 'oh'. Exquisite pleasure tinged with pain contorts her pretty features. Her eyes go distant, like she's being transported to another plane of existence by the sheer force of my cock.

I rear back, letting my shaft slide almost completely out of her. My length emerges dripping before I ram back into her hard, making her cry out. I wrap an arm around her so I can grope her tits while I fuck her from behind. I pinch and twist her nipples, making her shudder with tortured delight. Sweat glistens along her perfect arching spine, and I lean in to lick it off. Hartley shivers as I taste the salty bead, loving the way she pushes her body for me. After the night we've had, I know my sweet girl must be exhausted, but she doesn't let it show. In fact, the harder I pound her pussy, the harder she fucks me back. Her cunt clenches tight around me as she comes again, whimpering incoherently while her legs drip with honey. Even my own thighs are wet with her come, adding lubrication to each violent thrust. I take her hard and fast, letting my wild desires take over. I don't have to hold back, not with her. Hartley is the only woman on the planet who can meet me, push for push. Even when her pussy lips are shiny and rosy with friction, when she's drenched in come and sweat, when she can't remember her own name—she remembers one thing: she belongs to me. Her body opens up for me alone.

"No one else can make you come like this," I growl.

"Nobody. Never," she gasps.

My fingertips dig into the pillowy softness of her ass. Her flesh is silky smooth, and I can already see tiny, round yellow bruises blooming under her skin. We are perfectly matched in our contrast—me, hard and sharp. Hartley, soft and abiding. For me, she bends when other women would break. For me, she is a goddess, a pristine vessel for me to fuck and fill with my seed. Fate has brought her to me, but I would face a battle like today every day until the end of time to keep her here. Even if it meant changing every-thing, I would alter the universe to put us together again every single time.

I was so close to losing her, and I'll never let that happen again. Now that we're here, Hartley is mine. With every kiss, every grip, every command I remind her of that.

I pull back and slam into her hard, making her whole

body shake as I start to lose control. She drops her head back onto my shoulder. She's panting and murmuring some jumbled-up combination of my name and nonsense words. I smirk as I fuck her harder, loving how easy it is to work my girl up into hysterics. My cock has made her damn near delirious, just gasping for breaths in between earth-shattering thrusts. My balls slap against her ass, my shaft buried so deep inside of her, we're almost one being. I rock my hips so that I slam into her g-spot again and again. The look of dizzy bliss on her face tells me I hit it every time. I feel my balls grow heavy. The tension peaks, and all remaining semblance of control disappears. My cock rams into my sweet captive hard, losing rhythm as I move faster and faster. I slide my hand up to grasp the collar at her throat.

"I'm going to fill you up," I hiss. "I'll make it so everyone knows you're mine."

"Yes, oh god, yes," she gasps.

"You need it, don't you? Just like I do," I growl.

Hartley whimpers, "I need it. Please."

With a few more shuddering thrusts, I spear into her pussy and hold there. The most incredible high passes over me, my whole body ringing with the power of my orgasm. I feel my balls twitch, emptying every last drop of my seed inside of her. Hartley's glorious body clenches tight and I feel her climaxing around me, squeezing her honey down her legs along with mine. I rut into her a few more times until my cock is fully spent. I release her collar and slip my arms around her, kissing her hair, her neck, her back. I hold her through the shockwaves of glowing pleasure. We tremble together, covered in sticky come and breathing hard.

When I finally withdraw, I feel a trickle of my come gush down her legs. I zip myself up and gently turn Hartley around. Her pretty face is flushed, making the blue of her eyes stand out even more. Her blonde hair falls in messy tangles around her face. Her beautiful body glistens with sweat and accentuates every crease and curve. She's a work of art, meant for me to admire.

I lean in and kiss her. When I pull back, she's smiling. Her eyes shine with admiration. I cup her precious face in my hands and murmur roughly, "Don't you leave me again. I'm in love with you, Hartley."

With those blue eyes still locked on mine, she gently turns to kiss my palm. She leans into my touch and gives me that dazzling smile. There's no hesitation when she replies in a sultry, soft voice, "I'm not going anywhere. I love you too."

CHAPTER 28

HARTLEY

I hum along with the radio as I drive down a quiet road on the outskirts of Brighton Beach. My new silver Mercedes purrs quietly around a corner and a swell of sunlight floods across the windshield. I put on my designer shades and enjoy the warm sun on my face. It's a beautiful day in March, with the snow melting away to reveal the green earth waiting to grow again after the winter months. It's still quite cold outside, but I'm perfectly bundled up in a baby blue sweater dress, white peacoat, woolly tights, fleece-lined boots, and a thick-knit beanie. The last item I am particularly proud of, since I made it with my own hands. Learning to sew and knit are just a couple of the skills I have been sharpening over the past few months.

After that fateful last encounter with my parents, I had a change of perspective. Suddenly, I could walk freely in the city without the fear of being captured. My thoughts were no longer consumed by my past. I could actually think about my future, something that always seemed clouded in fog before. When I was living in the Bronx as Maggie, I thought I was free. But the paranoia that my family would track me down and lock me up again kept me from trying new things. I was getting by, but I was still a captive of my own fear.

Now, I feel confident that Zakhar will protect me. Not only that, but he has taken so much time and effort to teach me how to protect myself, too. Nearly every day, he leads me in another informal self-defense course. He teaches me how to throw a punch and how to evade one. He shows me the proper way to carry and handle a firearm. With the added advice of the Bratva doctor, we've studied how to make a tourniquet, how to perform CPR and chest compressions, and even how to stitch a wound closed—in and out of the field. My lover is a font of information. He has seen and experienced so much in his lifetime, and I am eternally grateful to him for passing along those life lessons to me.

Unlike my father, who denied me access to knowledge so he could keep me in the dark, Zakhar cares about my mind as well as my body. With his help, I've re-enrolled in university, this time studying the Russian language as a minor along with my culinary major. It's a joy to take the lessons I learn in class and turn them into something useful at home. I get a thrill every time I learn a new traditional Russian recipe—especially when Zakhar gives it his stamp of approval and authenticity. And learning to tell him how I feel in his own language is a gift for both of us, not to mention an investment in our future together. It's vital that we understand each other on the deepest soul level. We are a team, and a damn good one at that.

Today is Sunday, and I'm out and about picking up

special ingredients for a traditional Russian meal I want to cook for Zakhar tonight. There was a time when I would have feared going out alone like this. But I've grown up a little bit. I'm not a frightened little girl cowed by her father anymore; I am a brave, strong woman empowered by her lover's support. He's taught me how to look after myself. I'm not afraid when I park my Mercedes and step out into the crisp air alone. I'm still humming the radio tune as I grab my reusable tote bag and make my way around the corner to my destination.

It's a hole-in-the-wall artisanal goods shop in a small town outside of Brighton Beach, known for its eclectic and hard-to-find Old World ingredients. There are spices, teas, and even produce I couldn't pick up at the local grocery store. There's also a special kind of chocolate sold here that Zakhar recently admitted in passing to be his favorite. With his birthday coming up in a couple weeks, I'm on the hunt for treats and items that will remind him of home. I doubt he's had anyone make a big deal of his birthday in a long time, maybe ever, and I intend to go all out.

The bell over the door jingles as I walk in. I pick up a basket and smile at the old woman perched behind the counter. She gives me a nod and turns back to her Russian-language newspaper. Soft European pop music plays overhead. I meander down the short aisles, admiring all the unusual packages. I take my time searching out my list of ingredients. I'm happily studying the nutritional facts of a bag of pasta, parsing out which Russian words I can decipher, when I hear a man clear his throat one row over. It's just an innocent noise, but something about it makes the hairs on the back of my neck stand up. There was a time when I would ignore it, but Zakhar has taught me to trust my instincts. He's also taught me the art of silence.

I manage to quiet my breathing down to almost nothing, centering myself as I take tiny, silent steps toward the end of the aisle. Clutching my basket tight, I slowly lean around the end, poking my head out just enough to peer with one eye down the other aisle. There's a tall, slightly stooped man in a black trench coat. He's standing in front of a display section of dried rose petals, but I quickly realize he's not looking at the flowers. He's looking down at a cell phone with a sour look on his face. I startle a little at his appearance—the man has the distinctive puffy look of someone who has undergone plastic surgery. And judging by the look of it, either he got it at a discount, or the doctor had his work cut out for him. His nose is oddly flattened and shiny, and there's an irregularity to his lip shape. There's a raised scar along his jaw that almost looks like a seam. And yet, underneath it all, the visage is familiar to me.

When he turns slightly toward me, I see that scar extend down the side of his neck. My hand twitches at the memory of plunging a heel into that neck.

It's Evgeny.

I slip back around to my own aisle, trying to keep my breaths level while my mind goes in a million directions. How is this guy even alive, much less brave enough to show his beat-up face anywhere near Brighton Beach? I remember the last time I saw him… when he and his loyal chauffeur leaped from the Pakhan's balcony. I recall staring down into the dark at his body, unnaturally bent and twisted from the fall. He wasn't moving then, but he's clearly alive and well now. I look again and see that the man's eyes are darting around suspiciously. His hands are in his pockets with his coat wrapped tight around him. I watch from afar as he shuffles up to the counter and murmurs something to the woman. She doesn't ring anything up for him. Instead, she pulls out a thick envelope from under the counter and slides it across to him. The man takes it and walks out of the shop, leaving the old woman to watch him with a defeated expression.

The urge to question her is tempting. But Zakhar has drilled it into my head not to involve innocent people if I can help it. Simply interrogating that woman could put a target on her back, and that's not worth the risk. Still, I can't just let Evgeny slip away like that. Zakhar and I have been operating under the assumption that he was dead. If he's still alive, he's still a threat—to Zakhar, to me, to the brotherhood at large. I can't only think of myself; being Zakhar's fiancée requires me to think about the greater picture.

He belongs to the Bratva, and I belong to him.

So I quickly make my purchases and hurry out of the shop, keeping my knit beanie far forward on my head and my coat collar rolled up for extra anonymity. I see Evgeny take out his cell phone and press it to his ear. I can't hear what he's saying, but he's in a hurry. I keep back a small distance and watch him get into a weathered-looking black Honda on the driver's side. At least that means his trusty chauffeur probably isn't in the picture anymore. One less enemy to consider, I think to myself.

As his car pulls away, I consider dropping the whole thing and just going back to the warm, light-filled loft apartment I share with Zakhar. He'll be home soon, and we can curl up on the sofa together or, better yet, in bed. I can let his fingers roam my body and erase the memory of Evgeny's scarred countenance. But a sense of duty compels me to follow the bastard. I have to know for sure what I'm dealing with before I get Zakhar involved. Besides, he's already off on his own mafia business, and he's trained me very well. Perhaps I can handle a little more heat on my own now.

The adrenaline is starting to flow when I get behind the wheel and pull off down the road after Evgeny. My silver Mercedes is the perfect vehicle for this—Zakhar selected it for me especially for its quiet engine. It hardly makes a sound as I creep along, going farther out on Long Island as the sunlight wanes in the sky. I cut my headlights to avoid being seen. I can just barely see the Honda far ahead, and I make sure to stay back. Evgeny won't recognize the new vehicle, and probably won't see me behind the darkly-tinted windows, but I'm cautious anyway. With every mile that ticks by, that little voice in my head nags me to call Zakhar. I don't like keeping secrets, even little ones, from him. But I'm so focused on the slow and steady chase, I keep my hands on the wheel and my eyes on the speck of a Honda far ahead of me. The weather is clear, but the light is depleting, and there's still slick patches along the road, so I use extra caution. I follow Evgeny for almost a half hour, until he finally pulls to a stop in front of an old warehouse. I stop half a block back and turn off the car so I can survey the scene.

The building is falling apart, with sections of brick missing to expose the metal framing beneath. The lot itself is extremely overgrown. Grass and weeds poke through the melting snow. A flock of crows perch ominously in the dead tree out front. The warehouse looks like it hasn't been touched in years, but Evgeny strolls right up to the dilapidated entrance and walks inside. I bite my lip nervously, but decide to park and follow him in. I'm not the same girl who clunked her way through the air vents at the Pakhan's mansion months ago. I move with stealth. I stick to the shadows and drag my footsteps through the snow to prevent leaving a perfect trail. I inch along the outer wall, keeping my hand in my pocket. My fingers rest on one of my Christmas presents: a switchblade in a pretty pastel pink shade.

I hear men speaking inside as I approach the entrance. Someone asks in Russian, "Did you collect the money?"

I'm grateful for the Russian lessons Zakhar has given me.

In English, Evgeny responds, "Without a hiccup."

"*Khorosho*. Pity we have to do it this way."

Evgeny scoffs, "Not for much longer. We've been careful this time. Building our offense in secret. The fewer of us are involved, the better."

"The fewer to share the bounty with."

"*Da*. Precisely. Alexeyev may have taken out many of my most loyal Brodyaga, but he failed to eliminate me. As much as I would love to surprise him, it has been useful flying under the radar."

"I suspect he's still distracted by that little whore."

"No doubt about that," Evgeny spits bitterly. "It's unfair, you know. Fate has already granted that man so many advantages, *and* he gets the girl, too."

"Forget about her. We would rather have cash than cunt."

Evgeny cackles. "Right you are. And now that the Derzhatel obshchaka is on our side, I can finally get out from under the Pakhan. What a disgrace to have to turn on the man who commanded us all. But when Alexeyev is his vicious lapdog, what choice do I have?"

"You mean 'we'."

There's a beat, and then Evgeny adds quickly, "*Da, da.* Of course. *We.* When I rise, we all rise together. Anyone loyal to me will escape the falling hammer."

"And the rest?"

"They will be dealt with. I—we—coordinated that arrest on Coney Island. The cops on payroll are a step behind us. Any man who doesn't fall in line with the new order we establish will end up behind bars. Or worse," he adds greedily.

By now, my mind is reeling. I thrust my hand into my other pocket, fumbling for my phone so I can text Zakhar. He needs to know what's going on. This is beyond my control. When I finally fish out my phone with a trembling hand, I notice the screen light up. And then, before I have time to react and prevent it from happening, my phone starts ringing.

At top volume. In the middle of the silent backcountry.

I hastily answer it and press the phone to my ear by reflex just as I hear the men inside running to the door.

"Hartley?" asks Zakhar's voice with genuine concern.

There's a burst of gunfire, and I scream.

Chapter 29

Zakhar

The sound of Hartley's scream pierces through me like a hot knife. It's so loud, I instinctively hold the phone out away from me at first.

"Hartley? Hartley!" I shout into the phone.

I hear a soft crunching sound, then more muffled screams and… something else. Too deep in tenor to belong to Hartley. It's male voices shouting. I press the phone hard to my ear and listen intently with my heart pounding. Arseny looks over at me, confused.

The two of us have been carrying out routine interviews and check-ins with our various mafia watchdogs placed strategically across the state of New York. Currently, we stand in the foyer of a modest old farmhouse belonging to a long-time mafia contact out on Long Island. The resident of the house is a mid-ranking member with close ties to the Pakhan himself. Today, we are visiting him for another regular check-in, to catch up on the data he's collected, the sightings he's seen, and fill him in on new developments. He's our last stop of the day.

We were finishing up the interview, just shooting the breeze, and I decided to give Hartley a call. I miss her, even though I kissed her goodbye just this morning, and I wanted to tell her I would be heading home soon.

Plus, I felt a strange nagging feeling that something was off. That I needed to check on my beautiful love, make sure she's home safe. Instead, I heard that horrific scream.

"Did you hear that, boss?" Arseny asks, coming up beside me with a grim expression. "Maybe it's the wind, but I could've sworn I heard a woman scream."

"Which direction?" I demand.

He jerks his head to the east. "That way, I'm pretty sure. Who's on the phone?"

"Hartley," I admit, already striding out of the farmhouse toward my black sedan and his motorbike parked on the roadside. Arseny runs to catch up with me and thrusts his keys at me.

"If that was Hartley I heard, you need to get to her fast," he says. "Take my motorcycle. Fuck the speed limit. Fuck traffic laws. Go get your girl."

I give him a meaningful nod of gratitude, take his keys, fit the sleek black helmet on my head, and climb atop the motorcycle. It's been a while since I drove one, but as soon as I rev the engine, that old muscle memory comes back. The bike peels off down the darkening highway. I don't hang up the phone, but tuck it into my jacket pocket opposite my gun.

The sun is going down fast on this late winter evening, and I only have a matter of time to find Hartley somewhere out here, close enough to hear her scream, but she could be anywhere. A beautiful needle in an endless haystack. I don't know what's happening to her, but I know time is not on my side. My eyes scan the graying landscape as the bike barrels down the road. I break eighty, ninety, one hundred miles an hour. The cool wind whips around me, but I feel nothing—only the pounding, demanding need to find Hartley and save her.

I'm starting to lose hope as I watch the fields and forests roll by, empty of any signs of human life. The occasional car honks at me as I speed past, barely caring if I live or die in my haste to reach Hartley. It's only when I hear another scream—this one much closer—that I realize I'm almost there. Through the rumble of the motorbike, the whistling wind, and my own chugging heartbeat, I hear my lover's voice high-pitched and clear.

And full of distress.

Driving more by instinct than conscious thought, I whip the bike around a corner and finally set eyes on an old, tumbling-down warehouse with an overgrown lawn. Foggy memories of visiting this warehouse on mafia business years ago, when I was still a young recruit, drift back to me. It was just another low-profile location to store weapons and supplies, hold interrogations, make drops, and detain hostages. As far as I can recall, the place fell into disrepair once the current Pakhan took power and the owner of the warehouse got the hell out of dodge. Driving by, I would hardly notice the building if I didn't have the vague memory it was there.

But there's movement in the yard that draws my eye, even from the road. My eyes adjust to the low light just in time to make out the shapes of two large men hobbling across the weedy lawn. They move with the posture of hunters stalking their prey. They whirl around at the rip of the motorcycle engine, distracting them for just a moment before they return to their hunt. About twenty feet away from them is a smaller shape trying to escape them.

My heart knows who it is even before my eyes do. My adrenaline kicks into overdrive. I slam on the brakes of the motorcycle, eliciting a squeal from the tires on the icy asphalt. I leap off the bike and land on the pavement. I keep low to the ground and move as quickly but silently as I can, straight for Hartley.

My girl looks so tiny compared to the men stalking her. She's dressed for an afternoon of leisurely shopping, not a brawl. She hasn't seemed to notice my arrival; she probably thinks she's alone out here. And yet, her stance is not one of fear. She isn't cowering. On the contrary, Hartley is brandishing her little pink switchblade like it's a sword and screaming half-coherent threats at the men even as they back her across the lawn. Her eyes are fierce, her expression defiant. Her whole body jolts with every threat she hurls at them. She's a hellcat, backed into a corner and spitting mad.

"Keep back! I swear I'll stab you like I did last time!" she screeches.

"You little bitch! It took me *months* to recover from what you did! Not to mention you cost me my best driver!" shouts the rough, unmistakable voice of Evgeny.

I freeze up for a moment. I expected—and hoped—to never hear that voice again after his leap from the Pakhan's balcony. I saw his broken body. I assumed he was dead.

A mistake I won't make twice.

"This is Alexeyev's *suka*?" cackles the other man. "What a nice surprise."

Although the years have aged him considerably since

the last time I saw him, I recognize him as the owner of the warehouse, who went AWOL when the current Pakhan took reign. The man must have been hiding out in some cobwebby, filthy hole somewhere, waiting for an opportunity to rise up against the Pakhan.

"I belong to Zakhar, and he'll kill you if you touch me," Hartley hisses.

A surge of pride joins the mess of chemicals pulsing through my veins.

"Not if he doesn't find out," Evgeny snarls. "I can hide you somewhere he'll never look."

"Like six feet under. We clean up after ourselves," adds the old man crudely.

Each of them raises a gun. My heart stammers over a beat.

Hartley stops abruptly, as though rooted to the spot. Her chest heaves with panicked breaths but my girl doesn't look away. She stands stock-still with that switchblade in front of her and stares them down, almost like she's daring them to do it. Even in this dire moment, she maintains her composure and looks death in the face with defiance.

All my instincts are trained on eliminating the threat to the one person most precious to me. Rage burns hot in my chest, but I let it fuel rather than distract me. My hand is on my gun. My fingers follow its shape with natural ease, slotting into place with the trigger poised. I have the element of surprise and the advantage of being an excellent shot. But the truth remains that I must aim true, or risk giving these guys the startle they need to fire at Hartley.

My senses sharpen as I commit to the act. Two kill shots. I have to get it right.

I move low to the ground and dart from one long tree shadow to the next. In the fading light, they don't even see me coming until it's too late. Evgeny and his henchman look at me in abject horror. I am close enough to see that scar on Evgeny's neck. Close enough to almost smell their fear as they realize death is imminent.

I lift my gun and fire twice. The men drop to the ground as the shots echo through the night air.

To my surprise, Hartley doesn't immediately run to me. In fact, she bravely walks right up to the bleeding bodies of the men. I watch her nudge them with her boot, then kneel down to check for a pulse on their wrists. When she's satisfied they're dead, she stands back up, turns my way, and bursts into tears as she runs straight to me. I catch her in my arms and swing her around, pressing her so tight to my chest I can feel her heart thumping away. I cover her face and head in kisses, stroking her soft hair, wiping away her tears.

"You came for me. I called for you, and you came," she sobs.

"I will always come for you," I promise.

"I'm sorry. I should've texted you the moment I saw Evgeny in that shop. I just thought… I don't know. I thought I could handle it," she confesses.

"You *did* handle it. You found the rot of the Bratva, and I shot them dead. It's over, my love," I tell her. "They're gone. You did it."

She pulls back and looks up at me with admiration. "*You* did it."

I smile down at her. "We did it together. As we do *all* things."

"What do we do about…?" she trails off, looking back at the corpses.

"I'll alert the Pakhan. A crew will arrive within the hour to clear the scene. It will be like nothing ever happened," I assure her. "We clean up after ourselves, as the old man said."

I take her hand and lead her back to the vehicles parked on the road. I follow behind her car on motorbike back to Arseny. I thank him profusely for the use of his bike. I make the call to the Pakhan, who is pleased to hear that two of his enemies have been eradicated.

My beautiful companion and I go home. We make dinner together. We slow-dance in the kitchen and share a bottle of wine, followed by a steamy hour or so in the shower together. We kiss, we make love, we fall asleep, we dream. And we don't spare a second thought for the evil men who almost kept us apart.

After Evgeny's death, the poison starts to slowly dissipate from our ranks. The Pakhan takes some time to reshuffle the chain of command. The old order, the hangers-on who followed Evgeny in hopes of collecting his scraps are gone. Gerasim is exonerated and brought back into the fold as a hero. Arseny is recognized for his loyalty and courage in battle. I am regarded with greater prestige than before, especially after I commit to several weeks of intensive extra training. The Pakhan puts me through physical tests of my strength and endurance. I take on new recruits, letting them shadow me as I perform my duties. I tackle the most impassible interrogation subjects and the dirtiest battles. I transport and protect huge sums of money. I spend over a month embroiled in whatever physical or psychological test the Pakhan can throw at me.

At the end of it all, I am rewarded with even more of the Pakhan's trust. Not only does he believe in me full-heartedly, but he accepts Hartley, too. She is no longer a threat to our security, no more a chink in my armor. Instead, she is the perfect complement to me. She's not just a damsel, but a capable woman deserving of her new prestigious position by my side in the organization. She supports me through every step of the training. Her belief in me never wavers, and she inspires me to new lengths and strengths.

One night, we're lying in bed together, basking in the afterglow. I'm stroking my lover's soft face, admiring her curves in the moonlight through the window. She glances up at me and smiles, and I'm overcome with love for her.

"You have changed a lot since the first time we met, *malyshka*," I murmur. "I felt from the start you were something special, but now… I know you are my perfect match. You are the companion I thought I'd never find. Our love is not a weakness; it makes us both strong."

"I wouldn't trade this life with you for anything," she says softly back.

"You know, we've waited a long time," I begin thoughtfully. "I have spent too long hiding our love. I am proud of us. I want the world to see you belong to me. Now that the dust has settled, I think it's time, my love. It's safe now."

She sits up and looks at me with wide, excited eyes. "Do you mean it?" she breathes.

I grin at her, running my thumb along her plush

bottom lip. "*Da*. I want to make you my wife. The two of us, always and forever," I assert.

She throws her arms around me and squeals with joy. I hold her close, rocking gently side to side as he buries her face in my neck. I feel as though nothing could make me happier—until I hear the sweetest words I've ever heard in my life come from my lover's lips.

"Well, it'll be the three of us, actually."

CHAPTER 30

HARTLEY

My heart is so full it could nearly burst. Everywhere I look, I find the smiling faces of well-wishers and new friends. It's a beautiful, warm Saturday afternoon in May, and nearly three hundred people have arrived at the Pakhan's mansion for the wedding reception. The stately old house has been filled with luxe decorations of white and gold. Streamers, banners, and ribbons adorn the walls and banisters. There are so many flowers, the air itself smells sweet. A live band plays jazzy love songs and classic dance tunes for the masses dressed to the nines. Men in black suits and smoking jackets, women in ballgowns and slinky lounge dresses fill the great hall.

It's so strange to think back on the first time I came here. The carnage, the confusion, the fear. That terrifying night feels like a lifetime ago. I have been back to the mansion several times since then. My incredible, strong, powerful man has elevated within the ranks. The Pakhan already trusted him, but now, they're thick as thieves. He invites us over for lavish dinners and nights of wild entertainment. With great reward comes responsibility. Zakhar is a natural leader in charge of a lot of important people. He's the eyes and ears of the Pakhan, but his muscle, as well. Of course, there are missions that take him from me for hours at a time, but I'm not just languishing without him at home. I keep busy with classwork as well as continuing the lessons Zakhar has taught me. Lately, I've been preoccupied with wedding plans and nesting for the baby, too. But every moment I can, I'm at his side. Truth be told, there's nowhere else I'd rather be. Anywhere with Zakhar is home for me.

He gives my hand a squeeze and I smile up at him. My lover is strikingly handsome in his black designer suit and tie. His dark hair is swept back from his face, and his soulful eyes survey the scene in between stolen glances at me. He is a stoic man of few words, and yet, he always finds a way to make sure I know how he feels. He tells me all the time how much he loves me, but even if he didn't, I can feel that love in every look and touch. Our bond is more powerful than anything I've ever known, and it feels so right to make it official tonight.

"Beautiful ceremony," says Arseny, a close friend and colleague of my husband. He looks handsome, too, in his fine suit. But no one can compare to my master.

"*Spasibo*," Zakhar replies, giving him a handshake. "You didn't fall asleep?"

Arseny chuckles. "*Nyet*. You kept it short enough. I'm sure your mother appreciated all those little traditions from the motherland, too," he points out.

"She insisted on making our wedding cake, you

know," I pipe up. "I tried to tell her it was too much, but she wouldn't take no for an answer."

"*Da*, that's the Galina I remember," Arseny says.

"And naturally, it turned out a thousand times better than anything we could've ordered from a caterer," I gush. "You can taste the love in every bite."

"*Matushka* adores you. Only the best for her new daughter-in-law," Zakhar rumbles. He leans over to kiss the top of my head. Arseny pretends to be disgusted.

"Congratulations to you both, but I have to hold a moment of silence for my *former* best bachelor friend. I thought we might be lone wolves for eternity," Arseny remarks.

"Love will catch up to you one of these days, too," I tell him with a wink.

Just as he's about to deny it, he's stunned to silence by a gorgeous young woman who comes floating up to us in a long, swishy gown. She looks familiar, but I can't quite place her. Zakhar gives her a polite nod, but Arseny gawks at her like he's never seen a woman before.

She congratulates us on our marriage, and then sweetly, quietly asks Arseny to dance. He trips over his words in his haste to say yes.

Zakhar and I can't hold back our laughter as Arseny is pulled away onto the dancefloor by this lovely newcomer. We watch the dancers take to the floor in pairs as a famous love song from the fifties starts to play. Even the Pakhan himself gives us all a happy surprise when he leads Zakhar's mother, blushing and trying to play it cool, into the crowd. It's a heartwarming scene, seeing all our friends and family gathered together to celebrate our love. Our wedding is a secretive affair; no one from my past knows about it, and Zakhar's mafia career demands secrecy even in these brightest moments. Beyond the booming live music, the smell of flowers and champagne, and the gilded walls of the mansion nobody even knows we're here.

But I don't mind. Our little world is enough for me. I have never been so happy, so sure that the future is worth living for. Tomorrow once felt cloudy, like a promise I couldn't trust the universe to keep. Now, I fall asleep with a smile on my face, confident in what's to come.

My joy only intensifies when Zakhar gently leads me onto the dance floor. He holds my hand in his, the other guiding the small of my back. Our bodies mesh together so perfectly, spinning in dizzy circles under the great crystal chandelier. My skin burns at his touch and I thrill at the thought of our wedding night. No matter how many times I come in his embrace, he always finds new ways to satisfy me. He is everything to me: protector, mentor, master, lover, and now husband. I have found my true match in Zakhar.

"Now, everyone knows what we've felt all along: that you and I are meant to be," Zakhar murmurs in my ear. His voice is rough, but soft—a special tone just for me.

"It's real now. No backing out," I tease playfully.

He cups my face in his hand, gazing into my eyes with pure adoration. I was only joking, but he looks at me like he's never been more serious in his life.

"I will protect you and our baby with every ounce of strength in my body. I promise to love and cherish you for all of time. You are mine and I am yours, and nothing can change that," he says fervently, as though our formal vows weren't promise enough. I feel the deep emotion behind his words. He means it.

"I know. And I promise to do the same. I love you, Zakhar," I whisper. "My husband."

"My wife," he says lovingly. I lean into his chest.

I close my eyes and smile, feeling his heartbeat against my cheek and our child's heart beating inside my womb. As we slowly spin across the dancefloor, we might as well be the only ones there. All the frills and music and conversation melts to background noise. There's nothing left to fear in this world, not when I'm wrapped in Zakhar's protective arms. My husband holds me close as we sway into the night, hopelessly, happily lost in the sea of love.

Thank you for reading! You may sign up for my newsletter to be notified when I have a new release on the way: http://alexisabbott.com/newsletter

~Alexis Abbott

CONNECT WITH ALEXIS

Get an EXCLUSIVE book, **FREE** just as a thank you for signing up for my newsletter! Plus you'll never miss a new release, cover reveal, or promotion!

http://alexisabbott.com/newsletter

facebook.com/abbottauthor

twitter.com/abbottauthor

instagram.com/alexisabbottauthor

amazon.com/Alexis-Abbott/e/B013YL5290

bookbub.com/authors/alexis-abbott

pinterest.com/badboyromance

ABOUT THE AUTHOR

Alexis Abbott is a Wall Street Journal & USA Today best-selling author who writes about dangerous men and the women who love them. If you can't resist a bad boy who is a good man, you just found your next addiction. With heart-stopping action, mouth watering sex, and passionate romances that will leave you breathless, Alexis Abbott writes romantic thrillers like no one else can.

When she's not writing your next book boyfriend, you'll find her living a real life romance novel with her own bad boy soulmate in Bonavista, NL, Canada.

Thank you for reading! You may sign up for my newsletter to be notified when I have a new release on the way:

http://alexisabbott.com/newsletter

~Alexis Abbott

---

facebook.com/abbottauthor

twitter.com/abbottauthor

instagram.com/alexisabbottauthor

amazon.com/Alexis-Abbott/e/B013YL5290

bookbub.com/authors/alexis-abbott

pinterest.com/badboyromance

Also by Alexis Abbott

<u>**Romantic Suspense:**</u>

Hitmen Series:

Owned by the Hitman

Sold to the Hitman

Saved by the Hitman

Captive of the Hitman

Stolen from the Hitman

Hostage of the Hitman

Taken by the Hitman

The Hitman's Masquerade (Short Story)

Heartbreakers MC

Breaker

Bones

Ironside

Big Daddy

The Killer Trilogy:

Book 1: Killer for Hire

Book 2: Killer Desire

Book 3: Killer on Fire

Hostages:

Trafficked

Stealing Her

The Assassin's Heart

Killing For Her

Abducted

Stolen Jewel

Possessive

KILLERS:

Hunter's Baby

I Hired A Hitman

STEPBROTHERS:

Ruthless

Criminal

GLITZ & GRIT:

Betting on Love

Vegas Boss

Rock Hard Bodyguard

Innocence For Sale: Jane

Redeeming Viktor

SEXY SEALS

Sweetheart for the SEAL

Sights on the SEAL

BDSM Romance:

Bound as the World Burns (SFF)

Acknowledgments

Thank you to my amazing Patrons. I'm constantly humbled and grateful for your support.

Ramona Cabrera
Melissa Hedrick
Virginia Swanson
Dawn Daughenbaugh
Don Doss
Stacie Currie

If you'd like to join them — and get my ebooks or paperbacks — you can find me here on Patreon.
https://www.patreon.com/alexisabbott